THE DAY THE STARSHIPS CAME

...was the day that man became a hunted
animal on his own planet. From the moment the
missiles failed to fire the human race was on the run.
But there was no place to hide, from—

THE HUNTERS

"It is one of those books that makes you want to know
more about the people, the situation, and 'what
happened next.' The characters are interesting and the
action sweeps you along—the only fault for me is that
there was not enough! Mr. Lovejoy is to be congra-
tulated. Another book on the routing of the masters
would be excellent."

—ANDRE NORTON

This is a work of fiction. All the characters and events portrayed in this book are fictional, and any resemblance to real people or incidents is purely coincidental.

Copyright © 1982 by Jack Lovejoy

A TOR Book

First printing, February, 1982

ISBN: 48-523-9

Covert art by: Thomas Kidd

Printed in the United States of America

Pinnacle Books, Inc.
1430 Broadway
New York, New York 10018

THE HUNTERS

—JACK LOVEJOY—

TOR

A TOM DOHERTY ASSOCIATES BOOK
Distributed by Pinnacle Books, New York

CHAPTER I: THE ANOMALY

It was twilight when the summons came. Disease, the wildmen, the terrible creatures that roamed the Barren Lands, made life precarious; those who strayed outside the Anomaly never returned. But the Old Man had survived all these.

Thelon had known death before; just two years ago his young wife and his father had died within a few days of each other, and he had never known his mother.

But this was different, like the crumbling of a mountain range or the drying up of the sea. The Old Man was his great-grandfather; he had been Mentor time out of mind. The summons could only mean that soon, perhaps within a matter of hours, he himself would be the last of the Carswells.

He followed the guide through the graying dusk. Both men were instinctively careful to avoid clearings in the forest, to use the foliage to screen themselves from the sky. They sought the shadows and were silent.

. Through the trees Thelon saw several gleaners, their reed baskets overflowing with the day's harvest. A band of poachers squatted in the underbrush nearby, waiting for night. Their hooded cloaks of bark and grass were cunningly sewn to resemble the land itself. Had they not waved as he passed, he would never have seen them.

The skycraft could somehow see even at night or through the densest fog. You never heard them coming; but they glowed faintly in the dark, giving an experienced poacher enough warning to fade into the landscape. In daylight the skycraft could be neither seen nor heard — until it was too late. But, of course, only a fool would venture into the Barren Lands during the day. Not even the wildmen did that.

Several young men hurried past in the opposite direction, away from the stockade. These had already deposited their filled gleaner's baskets, and were now wearing the hooded cloaks of the poachers. The strong had to assume a double load in food producing.

Although the Anomaly covered over a hundred square miles, there were nearly a thousand mouths to feed, and the long winter would soon be here. For a while there would be some ice fishing in the small lakes nearby; but these soon froze clear to the bottom. There were few animals abroad during the winter, and the mammoth game animals of the Barren Lands were always rounded up by the drover machines in late autumn and kept in the shimmering gray-green corrals until spring. In fact, the round-up was probably less than a month away now.

The short summer months were always a time of frantic activity. Even so there was often rationing and hunger toward the end of winter. The Anomaly was not a good place to live but it was one of the very few places where man could live at all. The Hunters owned all the rest.

The stockade was nearly three years old, though it was still in process of construction by the snydermen. Its gate seemed in the dim light to be no more than a dark patch of underbrush; the palisade looked like nothing more than a thick grove of trees. Even in winter the stockade's roof could not be distinguished from the rest of the boreal forest, especially from the air.

Thelon was only twenty-six years old, but this was already the fourth stockade to be built in his lifetime; the basic design had not changed in centuries; but sanitation and smoke absorption made it necessary to begin a new one every six or seven years. The stockades protected the people from marauding wildmen and the mammoth game animals that sometimes strayed into the forest from the Barren Lands. They were no protection against the Hunters, of course.

But the skycraft never appeared directly above the Anomaly. Why this was so, not even the Old Man knew. Nor did anyone know what the Hunters looked like. Over the centuries the legends surrounding them had grown more and more fantastic. Nobody really knew anything about the Hunters; only that they were deadly.

Each boy and girl was trained from earliest childhood in the norquist skills needed to survive in their harsh sub-polar world. Reading and writing had long been confined to the race of the Carswells. But all the people were confined within the boundaries of the Anomaly; there were certain hills and streams, the edge of a lake or a special outcrop of rock, beyond which the people never strayed. Not because they knew that these were the limits of a magnetic anomaly, but simply because they had never done so. They knew of the wildmen and the Indians — Tatoka was an Indian woman — but few suspected that there might be people like themselves anywhere else on earth.

Thelon suspected; although he had no real evidence. The Old Man had always been secretive and reluctant to share his hoard of knowledge, even with his own descendants, and so much that he knew would now die with him. It was only by chance that Thelon had heard the tale at all.

Both his father and grandfather were still alive at the time and he himself could not have been more than eight or nine years old. All four generations of Carswells had gathered in the Old Man's cabin, as they often did on long winter evenings, to read from his books and discuss with him what they had read. They had been talking about the drover machines, which looked like nothing so much as giant faces moving across the landscape as if by magic; they only appeared at the end of each hunting season. The huge animals were frightened of them, which made it simple for the machines to herd into the corrals for the winter. Some of the shimmering gray-green structures were over a mile square.

They had all known from their reading that man had once bred animals for similar purposes. The Old Man let slip the remark that the Hunters may have done the same thing with human beings: when he was a young man, a stranger had been found just inside the boundary of the Anomaly. Emaciated and feverish, he had never regained consciousness. But the Old Man had recorded his delirious tales of monsters and monstrous human beings. Thelon had never been permitted to see the manuscript, but he had never forgotten that chance remark.

He thought of that remark now as he approached the Old Man's cabin. The guide took his hand and led him through the maze of black trunks to the door. It opened on silent hinges, and Thelon stepped inside, where he felt rather than saw the presence of another person; only when the door and outer blackout curtain had been tightly closed did the person draw aside the inner blackout curtain. It was Tatoka, the wrinkled little Indian woman who looked after the Old Man. She seemed lost and bewildered.

The cabin was large and comfortable; the snydermen had filled its rooms with an amazing array of furniture and utensils. Centuries-old books lined one whole wall of the main room. The chess table, where Thelon had received so many defeats at the hands of the Old Man, had been pushed into a corner; the pieces were still set out in a last problem. And on a broad couch, beneath a thick quilt, lay the Old Man himself. Only the feeble rise and fall of the quilt showed that he was still alive.

Two girls of marriageable age sat nearby. They had come to help Tatoka tend the Old Man, but he was sleeping now. They used the time to practise their sewing. Thelon was over six feet tall — an unusual height nowadays — and strongly built. True, he had not shown much interest in women since the death of his young wife, but attitudes change. The two girls watched him out of the corners of their eyes as he knelt beside the couch.

Heavy white brows shadowed the Old Man's eyes; Thelon thought he saw the lids tremble, but he could ñot be sure. The breathing continued shallow and irregular. On the table lay an old medical book, closed; the Old Man had evidently found what he had been looking for. An old wooden chest stood on the far side of the couch.

"Yesterday morning, Thelon," said the old Indian woman, "he stopped reading in the big book there on the table. He put it aside and has not opened it since. Then he had us bring that wooden chest out of the storeroom. There are books and papers inside, and all day yesterday and through the night he went over them, sorting this and arranging that."

She stopped and corrected the way one of the girls was holding her needle. The girl blushed and lowered her eyes; it was several minutes before she could bring herself to look up at Thelon again.

Tatoka continued, "We left him alone because he wanted it so. But this morning I saw him crying. He has never wept in all the years I have known him, since your grandfather was a boy, Thelon. I had to turn away, and when I returned he was as you see him now."

The man who had brought the summons to The-

lon, a wiry grayish little man who did most of the
heavy work for Tatoka, was still standing by the
inner blackout curtain. "I gathered up the books
and things," he said. "Then I put them back in the
chest. Neatly, Thelon, neatly," he added quickly.
Like nearly all the people, he could neither read
nor write and had an almost superstitious awe of
books.

Thelon smiled and nodded at him, telling him
that he had done the right thing. He had no idea
what kind of books and papers were in the wooden
chest. The only times he had ever seen the old
wooden chest before was when it was being carried under the watchful eyes of the Old Man to a
new stockade. Naturally he was curious, but he
decided to wait until the Old Man awoke.

He knew that the two girls had been peeking
shyly at him whenever they thought Tatoka was
not looking. They were about fifteen or sixteen
years old, neatly and modestly dressed in the full
skirts and blouses worn by unmarried girls. The
styles were those of centuries ago, reproduced in
soft, finely-worked leather.

Nor would Thelon's trousers and jacket have
been out of place in one of the great cities of long
ago — except, of course, for the material. But soon
only he would know this. The people knew nothing
of great cities or the world of long ago; they lived,
worked, dressed, and thought exactly as their ancestors had for generations. Without a written language to maintain continuity, the spoken language
had changed, but little else had, time out of mind.

The handyman sat patiently down on a stool
near the door. Even Tatoka, after fussing about

the room for a bit, finally settled herself between the two girls to continue their sewing lesson. Despite the impending death — even a death of this magnitude — the norquist skills must be passed on lest the people die.

There was nothing any of them could do now but wait. Thelon himself sat down with a book in one of the well-crafted leather chairs, a respectful distance from the old man's couch. The book was Speke's *Discovery of the Source of the Nile*. Why he had selected this particular book at this particular time he himself probably could not have answered. The Old Man had always frowned whenever he saw him reading this book, or any of the other travel and adventure books on the shelves.

Thelon's father and grandfather had both been dutiful, unimaginative scholars; patiently learning long lists of vocabulary, memorizing names, dates, and systems of classification. But Thelon had always tried to comprehend the meaning and significance of whatever he read, rather than merely memorizing it. And he had asked questions, probing questions; especially about the world beyond the Anomaly. When he was young he had even questioned the wisdom of merely transferring the same mechanical skills from generation to generation. Such heresies were quickly suppressed by the combined weight of three generations of Carswells. Thereafter he had kept his questions to himself. But he had not forgotten them.

Nor, evidently, had the Old Man. His shrewd old eyes had asked some probing questions of their own. Perhaps he had seen deeper into Thelon's heresies than Thelon had himself. In any case, the race of the Mentors had to be preserved; even if it meant going outside the direct line of descent of the Carswells.

Thelon had always dismissed his cousins Elwood and Gustavson as pimply young prigs. They drilled ceaselessly over a few select books; but with little understanding and less imagination. The Old Man had been satisfied with their development, however. He had made only token objections when Thelon had taken the unprecedented step of moving out of the stockade after the death of his young wife.

There were still some ragged old books in existence in the stockade, and even a few people who had somehow learned to read. Elwood and Gustavson had suggested that this sort of thing should be discouraged. The suggestion had not displeased the Old Man; although he evidently thought that a few old cranks could do no harm. Such literacy as still existed was at best rudimentary. It would soon die out through natural processes.

Suddenly the Old Man gasped, a sharp rasping sound; his breathing became even more labored and irregular. Tatoka was instantly at his side. Everybody watched the couch apprehensively while the Old Man gasped for breath as if he were strangling. After a few frightening minutes he subsided once more into his former state.

They all sat back again, except the old Indian woman. Once more she began fussing about the room, snuffing the candles, sweeping up imaginary specks of dust and dirt. At last she hustled the two girls into the kitchen to prepare a meal.

Once more Thelon tried to read, but his mind wandered. He glanced at the big leather-covered ledger that registered every birth, death, and marriage among the people for centuries past. There were two entries under his own name; three under his dead wife's. There was no formal religion; just a ceremonial registration of the three major events in one's life.

It was like the world had been before the rise of true religions, Thelon mused. People did not pray for help from the gods, but merely performed certain rituals in hopes of warding off demons. But in this case the rituals had real meaning: never show a light at night, never venture into the open by day, never cross certain boundaries. And the Hunters were not mythical demons. They were real.

He was distracted from these thoughts by the sound of hushed squabbling in the kitchen where the girls were arguing, and unsuccessfully trying to do it inaudibly. Tatoka sighed and shuffled off to investigate. Instant silence; then, only the whispered scolding. Then more silence.

Thelon looked down at the shriveled figure on the couch, pathetically gasping out its last breaths of life. He knew that the Old Man had something to tell him, perhaps something important. Once more he glanced at the wooden chest, placed intriguingly on the far side of the couch.

The two girls were herded out of the kitchen by Tatoka; each held one side of a wooden tray that could easily have been carried by either but apparently some kind of compromise had been reached.

Carefully maintaining his own sobriety, he

thanked them as they set the food on the table
beside him. The girls blushed, and one of them
started to giggle. But a warning glance from
Tatoka silenced her. One of the girls then carried
the tray to the wiry little handyman and brusquely
shoved a plate at him. He grinned toothlessly at
Thelon as he took it, shaking his head at the eter-
nally absurd behavior of the young. The girls then
resumed their sewing lesson, but between stitches
they watched Thelon out of the corners of their
eyes, anxious to see if he approved of their
cooking. Fish broiled with wild herbs, stewed
greens and mushrooms, and a berry pudding; simple, but well prepared. Like all the people, the two
girls had been brought up to perfect a very limited
range of skills within a very confined existence.
They both would make good wives. Thelon nodded
at them, showing his approval of their cooking.
The girls flushed with pleasure, and applied
themselves to their sewing lesson with
renewed — and very obvious — dedication.

Hours passed, and still the Old Man did not
awake. There seemed little change in his condition, one way or the other. Thelon had at last settled down to his book; Tatoka and the two girls
continued the sewing lesson; the handyman dozed
on his stool. It was after midnight when they were
roused by a soft tapping at the door. Tatoka
frowned as she rose to answer it.

Elwood and Gustavson annoyed her; although
she had always been polite to them, in deference
to the Old Man she considered them pompous and
absurd. The twinkle in the handyman's eye showed that he thought so too; although his reaction

was more of amusement than annoyance. The two girls looked suddenly very bored.

There was an animated conversation in the entrance passageway, but the words were muffled by the thick blackout curtain. A moment later Tatoka slipped back into the room, looking more annoyed than ever. "It is Elwood and Gustavson," she said to Thelon. "But I see that you have already guessed that. When he" — she nodded toward the couch — "awoke this afternoon and sent for you he said that they were not to enter. Twice they have been here, and twice I have sent them away. And now they are back again. What am I to do, Thelon?"

He looked at the couch again, and at the mysterious wooden chest at its side. He thought he could guess why the Old Man had forbidden entry to his cousins. Since no one else of the household could read, the chest could be left safely beside the couch. But Elwood and Gustavson could read, and there was apparently something in the chest that the Old Man did not want them to see.

Thelon had never agreed with this secretive hoarding of knowledge. Whatever the Old Man wanted to tell him, it surely had something to do with the contents of the chest. He wondered now if it would ever be told. Meanwhile he saw no reason why his cousins — no matter how pompous and absurd they were — should not be permitted to pay their last respects to their dying teacher.

"Let them in, Tatoka," he said. "It was only that he did not want them here until I had arrived."

Her old eyes narrowed shrewdly. She had spent most of her adult life tending the Old Man's needs, almost like some pagan acolyte tending her god, and she knew his ways better than he knew them himself. The presence of the wooden chest was new, and so was the order to keep the two cousins out of the cabin. The connection was not hard to guess.

She held open the blackout curtain, and the two cousins stepped into the room, blinking at the light and bowing absurdly in all directions. They had both prepared speeches, but Thelon cut them short, with a curt nod toward two chairs in the corner; they could hardly have reached them little faster with a running dive. They were even more terrified of Thelon than of the Old Man. The little handyman chuckled; he had always been treated haughtily by this pair, and found their discomfiture a pleasing sight.

They sat silently in the corner for several minutes; then, little by little, they began to whisper. Soon they were preening themselves with bits and scraps of knowledge in the age-old manner of prigs. The two girls were decidedly unimpressed; all this book talk was to them just so much empty gobbling. But Elwood and Gustavson thought they were making a great impression, especially when they began to discuss the famous assassination of Julian by Brutus and "Castor."

What finally annoyed Thelon was the sheer futility of it all. This was the gathered knowledge and experience that had once raised mankind above the brutes and savages, the lore that had once inspired works of beauty and splendor and genius. The Old Man had been wrong; he was sure of that now. It was not enough merely to transmit the same knowledge and skills from generation to generation. There must also be curiosity and imagination, a continual reaching out for new horizons, the desire to understand. The Anomaly was only a very small part of the world. He glanced toward the corner.

Elwood caught his glowering eye, and immediately fell silent. Gustavson continued his empty chatter until he got a nudge in the ribs. He froze in mid-sentence, his mouth hanging comically open. Then both cousins grimaced and muttered apologies. The two girls did not look up from their sewing, but their lips quirked mischievously.

Except for an occasional word of advice about sewing, two hours passed before anybody spoke again. Then they all seemed to be talking at once. Thelon suddenly felt an unnatural stillness in the room; he looked up as the old Indian woman rushed past him to the couch; her wail of grief was heartrending. He had been summoned here to be told something, perhaps something of great importance. But now he would never know. The Old Man was dead.

Tatoka knelt beside the couch, moaning and rocking back and forth. The others were on their feet, all talking at once, milling aimlessly about the room. They shrank from the corpse with superstitious dread; the foundation of their lives seemed to be crumbling beneath their feet, and they did not know which way to turn. Thelon shared their feelings of awe; but somebody had to take charge of the situation.

He sent the handyman to the Chief Snyderman with orders to prepare a coffin. Then he got rid of

Elwood and Gustavson by sending them out to
make the announcement to the people; this would
be a great opportunity for posturing and self-
importance, and would keep them out of his way
for at least a few hours. The big problem was
Tatoka.

The two girls, at last conquering their dread of
the corpse, were now trying to help her to her feet.
But she pushed them away, her moans now giving
way to eerie wails of grief. There was a glazed look
in her eyes; tears streamed helplessly down her
leathery, wrinkled cheeks. Nothing the girls could
do seemed to make any difference.

Thelon spoke gently, relying on the sound of his
voice to quiet her. Then he assured her that she
was needed, to wash and prepare the body for
burial. Service to the Old Man had been the center
of her existence; here was a service she could still
perform for him, even if it was the last. She was on
her feet in a moment, scurrying about the cabin
for the things she would need to prepare the body.

The old wooden chest was lighter than Thelon
had expected. He carried it into the bedroom; then
returned for a reading lamp.

As the wiry little handyman had assured him,
everything had been put back neatly. There were a
few books, several handwritten manuscripts in
the Old Man's precise handwriting, and a bundle
of brownish printed columns, each preserved with
a film of wax. This last he recognized as ancient
newspaper clippings, although the last newspaper
had been printed centuries ago.

But the large manuscript that lay at the top of
the chest was not in the Old Man's handwriting.

Perhaps it was what he had been reading when Tatoka looked into the room and saw him crying.

He adjusted the reading lamp, and opened the yellowed manuscript with great care. The script was round and legible. Its title had been printed by hand. "Walter Carswell's Journal."

CHAPTER II:
WALTER CARSWELL'S JOURNAL

I've sat down here now every morning for three days, but I'm not a literary man and saying it doesn't come easy. Not that I haven't read my share of books; I have. A Forest Ranger gets plenty of chance to read. Especially during the winter when most of the roads are snowed closed. There's no television and not much radio because of the mountains, and not really too much to do. There are no tourists of course, and the bears are hibernating. Wolves and cougars have been getting scarcer for years now, and you don't even see many coyotes any more. Poisoned mostly, by the sheep ranchers. Can't arrest them either, because they swing too many votes at election time. But I'm wandering off from what I wanted to say.

A literary man would know how to type, but I don't. I've got a typewriter for reports and requisitions and such. But that takes too long, and people have always said that I've got a clear handwriting. Even my teachers used to say that. Besides, I don't really know how much time I've got left. The last radio station went dead a couple of weeks ago.

I once read that it's not so important how you say a thing as what you're saying. And I remembered that this morning, and decided to just put it down on paper and forget about trying to make it a literary masterpiece. So I ripped up the two and a half pages I'd already written (two days work, by the way) and I'm starting all over. With a different title, too. I had a whole list of fancy titles, like "The Invisible Death from the Skies" and "The Day the World Ended," which I think already is a book by somebody; and even, while my head was still spinning from trying to get the commas and adjectives all in the right place, "The Lone Ranger." A second look at that one and I saw what a fool I was making of myself. So this morning I decided to start over, and just call this "Walter Carswell's Journal," which is my name.

Like I say, I've read my share of books. Not literary books, but good solid stuff about the sciences, especially forestry and geography. So I was able to follow the reports on the radio and understand what was happening. When the whole East Coast got wiped out I naturally thought it was the Russians or Chinese. But as soon as I heard about the skytankers I knew that it couldn't be them. That would just be suicide. Since there's no television or newspapers up here I never did get a look at one of these tankers. All I got from the descriptions on the radio was that they were big.

There were lots of radio interviews (before it went dead) with anybody and everybody all trying to put in their two cents worth about what was happening. Football players, movie stars, and so forth, who didn't know what they were talking about. Just like advertising, and I paid no attention. But one interview I listened to was with the famous professor C.E. Peebles of Eddington Institute, which I think is in Missouri or Kansas somewhere, where many big names in science had gathered to work on the problem of the gas. Professor Peebles, I should add, is listed in several Department manuals and is considered a big man in the scientific community.

Now whoever did it picked the right place and the right time of year for it. For when Professor Peebles said in the interview that the skytankers were stationed at the top of the troposphere over the world's high-pressure zones, I knew at once what was happening. You see, the planet has several semi-permanent Highs, which means that the air descends out of them and spreads out (in the Lows of course it's just the opposite). These tend to move with the seasons. In winter they're usually over the continents and in summer over the oceans. In early spring they begin moving about, and that's when the first skytankers appeared. Of course this ruled out the Russians and Chinese because the world's strongest High is right over Siberia. We never did get any news from those two countries.

So the tankers had to be sent by somebody from another planet. I wondered at first why we didn't try to shoot them down with missiles. Or the

Russians, who also have missiles. There was nothing on the radio about anybody even trying. But then I realized that we probably did shoot all our best missiles at the skytankers and it didn't work. They were just afraid to admit it because people were already rioting and panicking enough as it was.

And of course they were moving, millions of them trying to get out of the way of the poison gases that were being pumped into the planetary wind system. But they didn't come up here. Most of the roads were still closed, but that wasn't the reason. You see, during the winter a big High settles right over this region, and so this would be the last place people would want to come. I worried about it myself at first. But no tanker came. Apparently whoever was doing it thought that there was nothing here worth bothering about.

In fact, that's apparently how they thought about the whole human race. They made no effort that I ever heard of to contact us, or talk things over. They just moved in and poisoned everything, the way the Department sometimes poisons a lake when they want to restock it with something else.

I had lunch and tried the radio again. Still nothing there. Reception is always better at night and I'll try again then. Spent some time checking over the supplies. My winter food stores are almost gone, but that don't bother me. I've got plenty of ammunition, and can live off the land as long as I have to. No problem there. But I can't do anything about the fuel.

In the old days a Ranger would cut his own fire-wood out of the forest. But some thirty years ago this place was modernized, with gas, electricity, telephone and all the rest of it. There's still the old fireplace though. And it's sometimes nice to light a fire at night, and relax with a pipe and a good book, with Duke (my dog) stretched out on the floor. But I'll need fuel-oil if I'm going to have electricity. The cooking-gas is almost gone, but that's just a convenience.

The telephone went out some three weeks ago. Not that it did me much good. I tried to call my sister in Maryland after it first started, but they told me that no calls were getting through to the East Coast. So Gloria and her husband and my little niece Jennifer were probably dead. I'm a bachelor and my parents died years ago, so I really didn't have anyone else to call. Later, when I tried to call down for news, they just told me to get off the line. But I will miss the electricity, which went out about the same time as the telephone. The auxiliary generator works fine, but the tanks are almost empty. The batteries for the radio won't last very long.

I have a whole shelf full of manuals sent out by the Department. Manuals on home vegetable gardening (seeds included), using wild plants for food, identifying mushrooms, and so forth. With summer coming on, the worst part about losing the electricity will be in preserving food. It would be a shame, for instance, to shoot a deer and then have Duke and me only get a couple of good meals out of it before it had to be thrown away. But I've got the Department's "Complete Guide to Home

Canning, Preserving and Freezing" on the shelf, so maybe I can figure out something. The snowline is only a thousand feet or so up. Maybe I can build an icehouse.

It is the next day now. I tried the radio for hours last night but no luck. In reading over what I have already written it strikes me that I sound rather casual about it all. Probably billions of human beings have been exterminated, and I sound no more unhappy than somebody whose golf game was rained out. This is not so. I said at the beginning that I was not a literary man. I suppose that is why it sounds so casual. I just don't know how to put down my sense of shock and loss and loneliness on paper. I'm sorry.

Of course I have read some of the many books about the last man on earth. Atomic bombs, radiation, biological warfare, mysterious plagues, purple clouds, poison belts, and all sorts of things wiping out all the people on earth. But I knew I was far from being the last man on earth. People who wrote such books didn't know much about geography. Not that I'm an expert myself. But I do know enough about wind and pressure systems to be sure that no matter how much poison the skytankers pumped into the atmosphere that there were sure to be hundreds of thousands, perhaps millions of people still alive. Besides, the gas was supposed to be very heavy and did not rise to high mountain regions like this. No, I was certainly not the last man.

How the other survivors are faring I don't know. I can't transmit on the radio and have no way of answering a distress call even if I should pick one up. So the best thing for me to do as far as I see it (and which is in fact my official duty) is to just stay put. For now, anyway.

Now the one thing we know about these exterminators is that they are more powerful than human beings. After all, they travel between the stars. It seems to me then that they should be more civilized than we are. I've seen ranchers stick a gas hose into a prairie dog village, and just wipe out thousands of dogs with the turn of a valve. And that's the way these exterminators treated the human race, with all its arts, sciences, books, buildings, cities, and so forth. Just like so many vermin! Is that what we are compared to them?

But I don't care if you're a god or just a monster; either way you don't go to the trouble of wiping out a whole planet without a reason. My guess is that they're here to stay, and soon as they get settled will probably start hunting down the survivors like me. But I think I can handle myself. There's not a man alive that knows these mountains better than I do.

Sept. 7 Beginning my journal again is almost as hard as it was to begin in the first place. In fact, so much has happened that I clean forgot about it. But I'm laid up for a couple of days (one of the youngsters dropped a hammer on it and it's swollen up so bad I can hardly stand on my ankle), and Brenda found this where I left it early last spring and said I should continue it. She says that it will be a valuable record someday, but I think I must have been making a nuisance of myself and she just gave it to me for something to do.

She agrees that I shouldn't worry about literary style but should just keep it like a captain would keep a ship's log. Which means of course more systematic, with each entry dated and so forth. She also says that I should identify myself for, as she put it, "the benefit of posterity." This seems a kind of conceited way of doing things, but Brenda is a college professor's widow and much more literary than I ever will be.

I was born in Silver Star, Montana (which is not far from Butte). Since last July 16, I am 33 years old. Height: 6'2". Weight: probably down to about 190 now after the summer's work and hunting (and fighting). Hair: brown. Eyes: same. Distinguishing marks or scars: old scar above right eye, new scar on left forearm barely healed. Education: graduate of Franklin High School (the one in Silver Star) and Eastern Montana A & M. Job: Forestry Service since I left college, Ranger for the last seven and a half years. Military: U.S. Marines, three year hitch.

This is pretty much the way I've always filled in an Accident Report, for instance when a tourist was brought in with an animal bite (usually another tourist's dog, but sometimes a bear or a snake), so now you have the "pertinent data" as Brenda would say. Now I will try and relate what's happened to me since I left off and bring everything up to date (although I'd much rather be out helping to build the stockade).

What stopped me from keeping up my journal was the sight of the skycraft. It was late in the afternoon and I was coming around the back of the cabin after checking the fuel tanks when I saw it. I call it "skycraft" because I don't know what else to call it. It didn't look much like a flying saucer or a science-fiction spaceship, and certainly not like any airplane I've ever seen. It didn't have wings or a tail or anything like that. I suppose I could describe it as shaped like a short, fat cigar, except hundreds of feet long. I thought at first that it was some kind of dirigible, like the Hindenburg that burned. When I first saw it, it was moving slowly to the southeast in the direction of Denver. Every few miles it stopped and just hung in the air like a helicopter, as if it was looking for something. Survivors, probably. And it was flying very low. In fact, since it was east of me towards the plains, I was actually above it most of the time and had trouble following it on account of the trees. I got out my binoculars and watched it until sunset when it disappeared from sight. It made no noise at all.

So they were on the prowl already, and I decided that I'd better start getting busy if I didn't want to get caught. Duke would have warned me of anybody coming on the ground. I know every stream, cave, game trail, and you name it for a hundred miles around. They wouldn't have caught me on the ground — at least I didn't think they would — but from the air, that was different.

I had learned some camouflage techniques in the Marines, and I set about the next morning camouflaging the cabin. That night I covered all the windows with heavy blankets. By the end of the week I was pretty sure that I could not be seen

from the air. For most of the way the little dirt
road that winds up here from the highway runs
through the trees. After I'd finished camouflaging
the cabin I dragged a lot of brush into the road, so
when the snow melted it would be hard to see
from the air. I replaced the blankets with blackout
curtains as soon as I had a chance to sew them. I
only lighted a fire in the early morning or late
evening when the mountain and valley breezes
were blowing and carrying away the smoke.

I saw the second skycraft the day after the electricity gave out. My camouflage passed the test,
for the skycraft went right overhead moving ever
so slow like it was looking around. Thereafter
hardly a week passed without my seeing one of
them. They came at different times of day. I don't
know if they came at night too, for they made no
noise at all. But I suspect they did. There must
have been a lot of them.

I've only seen one of the skycraft up close, and
that was just after I rescued Brenda and the
youngsters last May. I'll describe it in more detail
when I get to that part of the story, but I still don't
know what the people who are flying them look
like because I've never seen any of them. Neither
has Brenda nor any of the other twenty some
people we've collected over the summer, even
though some of them have seen the skycraft up
close and had close calls escaping. A lot of folks,
however, have been caught in the nets (which
more about later) and dragged up into the skycraft. God only knows what's become of them.

But I should really be more systematic in
keeping this journal, and will try and do so

tomorrow. That's all for now because it is getting
late.

Sept. 8 Most of last April I spent just getting
ready to survive. The snow was retreating up the
mountains and I got around more. My longest trip
was to the big watchtower five miles southeast of
here. In summer when there's danger of forest
fires they always have somebody stationed there
day and night (usually college kids). I had the key
so there was no problem getting in, but there was
nothing I could use in the building. I could see
nearly half the state from the top with my
binoculars, and every hour or so I'd climb back up
and look around.

About noon I saw a skycraft way off in the
distance, but it was going the other way. I knew
now that these skycraft could move very fast when
they wanted to, thousands of miles an hour, but
most of the time they moved like big dirigibles.

Before the day was over I saw the smoke of four
different campfires and counted seventeen
vehicles on the highways, all moving in this
direction. Now that there was no more poison gas
it seemed that a lot of the survivors had figured
out that this was probably the safest place for
them to be.

As I looked at it then (and I've had no reason to
change my mind), I was still responsible for the
welfare and safety of people coming into the
National Forest. I know that some would call this
idea ridiculous, since the Department did not exist
any more, nor the whole government for that
matter. But it was my job, and I intended to do it.

But I would have to be careful. Even when an efficient system of law enforcement existed we used to get a lot of people up here who were no better than wildmen.

But nobody, good or bad, would stand much chance of getting through the next winter unless I got them organized now. Only the hardiest Indians had managed to live here before the coming of the white man. With my weapons and knowledge (both in my head and in the Department manuals) I was better prepared to survive than any Indian, but the people coming here had always had everything done for them, and would have no idea how to survive. Even scavenging would be tough. There were only a few small towns for thousands of square miles and just two up here in the mountains, Hadley and Traxler. Then too I knew from experience that there were those from the big cities more vicious than any savage.

Problems with the fireplace. I'll have to pick this up later some time.

Sept. 9 Worked a good part of the night, but I finally got the chimney drawing properly. I think I overdid it with the camouflage. And now my ankle's worse than before. Might as well continue this, since I can't do much else.

Nothing much happened until the second week in May. Then all hell broke loose, and everything happened so fast that it's hard to remember the proper order. By then I was in pretty good shape. I put aside a case of canned foods for emergencies, and kept myself and Duke going by hunting. The electricity was gone and now the cooking gas gave out too. But I had some hurricane lanterns, candles, and all sorts of emergency equipment which the Department maintains at all its stations according to regulations. I read and reread the manuals at night, and tried my hand at preserving some of the meat. It turned out all right, though Duke would not eat it, and it used up most of my salt. But there's a big salt lick not ten miles from here so I wasn't worried about that.

I made a kind of chart where the people seemed to be settling. As might be expected, most of them stuck close to the cross-country highway that goes through the mountains about thirty miles south of here. My cabin is in a corner of the National Forest area beyond which it's mostly deserted basin and range country. So it was well into spring before anybody came my way. For some reason there were no skycraft here (at least during the day) at this time.

I had used my bow for hunting at first, not wanting to give myself away with a rifle. I used to belong to an archery club, and though I'm a bit rusty I can still make my living if I have to. But others had guns and were using them, and not just rifles: once while I was at the top of the watch-tower I heard a sound from the direction of Hadley (the nearest town) that even though it was faint could only have been machine-gun fire.

I was getting ready to start contacting people, but that stopped me. I decided to prepare myself first. I had camouflaged the dirt road leading up to my cabin so it couldn't be seen from the air. Now I spent some days camouflaging it from the highway, planting saplings and digging so that you

couldn't see where it joined the concrete road and
so forth. Nobody ever did find that road, and
nobody yet has found the cabin. We should be safe
after the first good snow.

Duke is part collie and part German shepherd,
and while not a real big dog (65 lbs. tops), he's
smart. He seemed to sense what was going on and
was always on the alert. But he doesn't do a lot of
barking and never dashes off into the forest. He
just tenses and looks a certain way and you know
he's spotted something. And that's what he did the
morning I first came into contact with the wildmen. Which is a good thing because otherwise I
would probably have stumbled right into the
whole gang of them.

Now to get to even the closest spot where I'd
marked down a possible campsite on my chart I
had to pass close to Hadley. That was the direction
from which I'd heard the machine-gun fire. It was
then the middle of May and the snow was gone.
Everything was turning green and the wildflowers
were starting to bloom. So I took Duke with me
and headed down the mountain.

Hadley's a little place, (pop. 527) that sits near
the head of a long valley that opens out onto the
main part of the National Forest. I was kind of
curious to see what was going on there because I
knew a lot of the folks who lived there. The town
sits about a mile past the watchtower, which made
it about six miles from my cabin, but with winding
back and forth (I stayed away from the highway) it
was a trip closer to twice that distance. But I'm a
strong walker and having started at dawn it was
still morning when I came within sight of it.

A big hogback which they had to cut through when they built the new highway blocks the view from the watchtower, so I had to be nearly on top of Hadley before I could see anything even with my binoculars. What I saw looked like the morning after in Hell. I was angry at first and had my hand on my rifle when I thought of what must have happened to the poor folks who had lived there.

None of them were in sight anywhere. Just hundreds of the type we call "wildmen" now. A lot of them had motorcycles, and women of the same type with them. Though it was still morning many were already (or still) drunk. I almost hoped that one of the skycraft would fly over and spot them.

But there were too many for me to handle. At least, for the present. When I had collected as many of the decent folks as I could find, then it might be different.

An old game trail skirts the town. This took me about three miles out of my way and it was afternoon before I got back near the highway. Traxler (pop. 1,409) was the next town, about twelve miles down the road. I had a full pack but had no intention of going so far on this trip.

Sept. 10 Like I said, it was Duke who warned me. We were moving through the trees, trying not to get too close to the highway, when suddenly he stiffened and his ears went up. He looked at me in the way he does when it's people and not a bear or deer or anything like that. I had him sit, and slowly crept forward to investigate. The trees were not too dense here but a small outcrop blocked the way so I couldn't see who it was. I didn't want to turn the corner and run smack into a gang of wildmen so I started looking for a way to climb to the top of the outcrop. But then I heard the sound of a motor and saw a big gray camper coming straight towards me up a steep grade. It was moving slow and cautious.

Then I hear voices just on the other side of the outcrop. Sounded like about five or six of them all giving each other orders at once. And now I could see what they were up to. The highway made a hairpin turn less than twenty yards away, and there was a barricade right around the bend where someone coming up the road couldn't see it. It was an ambush and the gray camper was coming right for it.

I slipped off my pack, unslung my rifle and stuck a spare clip in my belt. The camper was almost to the ambush when I stepped around the outcrop. There were seven of them, two were young women. They were just heading for the road when I appeared in front of them.

"Right there!" I ordered them to stop and drop their weapons.

Three of them had shotguns and one a pistol but they were so startled that they obeyed. Also they looked in pretty bad shape from drinking and drugs and so forth. After they dropped their weapons, for a long minute they just stood staring at me. I stared right back.

And what a crew they were! Dressed in odds and like Neanderthals who had wandered into a war surplus store. Two months since it all started and we were already back in the Stone Age.

I was just going to order them to back away
from the weapons when I heard some yelling and
whooping from the highway behind me.
Instinctively I started to turn, and that was just
enough for one of them to dive for his shotgun. I
had no choice but to shoot him and another one
who also tried to pick up his pistol. Then the two
women started crying and screaming. The men
turned and ran off into the trees leaving the
women and casualties behind. Then I heard the
sound of shooting from the road.

I had to push the women out of the way (they
both looked paralyzed with drugs and fear) to
collect the weapons, which of course I could not
leave behind with them. Then I turned and headed
for the road.

The gray camper had been stopped by the barricade and had apparently tried to back up. But a
green pickup truck had pulled across the road
behind it, blocking the way. (It had been behind a
spur and I had not seen it.) There were five more of
the gang now attacking the camper, whose driver
backed hard into the pickup trying to shove it off
the road. The camper seemed to be heavily loaded
and the driver might have succeeded except that
one of the gang ran around to the front and fired
several bullets through the windshield. The
camper stopped dead.

They all screamed in triumph like savages and
one of them began smashing in the front windows
with a poleaxe while another shouted into the
trees for those I had just chased off. Suddenly
there was a shot from inside the camper and the
one smashing the windows dropped like a sack

with a bullet through his head. The others shrieked with rage and a young man with long hair and beard ran back to the pickup.

He came running back a minute later with a machine-gun, screaming obscenities, but before he could use it I shot him dead. I shot two more of them, including the one who had shot the driver, and the other two dove into the pickup and drove away. Then I hailed the camper, and came out where they could see me. I was wearing my Ranger uniform and I left my rifle at the side of the road with the weapons I had captured. But I stayed at a distance where it would have taken a good shot to have hit me and I was ready to duck for cover at the first sign of a gun.

The windshield of the camper was all spider-webbed with cracks and it was dark inside so I couldn't see anybody, not even the driver, who had certainly been shot. I hailed them again, and a face peeked out from a corner of the smashed wind-shield. A minute later the door swung open and a boy of about ten stepped out. He was crying. But he had a small-caliber pistol in his hand so I made no move towards him. Instead, I called him to me. Slowly and uncertainly he came forward. Then another boy a couple of years younger climbed down out of the camper door and stood staring at me.

"He's dead." The boy wiped his eyes with the back of his hand. "Are you a police officer?"

"Kind of," I answered, and as far as I knew I was the last representative of government in this part of the world. "Better put up that gun and show me what happened."

He hesitated a moment and then put the gun in his pocket. The older one's name was Mark, and it was young Randy standing by the camper door. Though city-raised they have both worked hard building the stockade (although Randy dropped a hammer on my ankle which is the reason I am writing this now in the first place). Both boys were dressed in bluejeans and denim jackets. I figured having something to do would be good for them, so I posted them as lookouts — besides, I would want to know if the gang I had chased off came back.

Brenda was sitting on the floor at the front of the camper, holding the head of her dead husband across her lap. Tears were running down her cheeks. The man, like Brenda herself, had been in his early thirties. He had been shot through the neck and forehead. His glasses lay next to him on the seat. Brenda just stared at me with a kind of blank look in her eyes. She was the one who had shot the gangster, but as she told me later she had acted in desperation; she had never fired a gun before. But the gang was almost sure to be back, and though we were a couple of miles from there, sounds carry a long way up here in the mountains and some of that Hadley crew might come here to investigate.

Now Brenda is a very well-educated woman with college degrees from big universities (certainly much bigger than Eastern Montana A & M), and even though badly stunned and scared she saw that we could not waste time or we'd all be dead.

I carried the body to the back of the camper

which was crammed to the roof with books. There must have been thousands of them, accounting for the heavy ride of the vehicle. Then I had Mark and Randy collect my pack and the weapons I had left by the side of the road, and whistled for Duke who came immediately. I set the boys to look after their mother and took the wheel of the camper. There was only one road up to the cabin and that passed through Hadley, so we couldn't go that way. The pickup had driven the other way, towards Traxler, but we had to get out of the vicinity fast and so I drove off in the direction of the pickup.

That's about all for now. My ankle's better, though still puffy, and I think I'll test it out tomorrow. Don't know when I'll get back to this.

CHAPTER III:
WALTER CARSWELL'S JOURNAL
CONTINUED

Sept. 26 It's raining cats and dogs and so I can't get out. I see in reading back that my last entry was a long one and it was over two weeks ago. Not really very much has happened since then. My ankle is fit again, and I've been helping with the stockade but mostly hunting and teaching the youngsters to trap and fish. With winter coming on this is important, for the women led by Grandma Norquist who is a farmer's widow can put up as much food as we can bring in. Grandma Norquist knows a lot more about canning and preserving and so forth than the Department manual, which she sniffs at. We're lucky to have her.

And here I'd like to put down the gratitude of all of us to Bob Snyder, who is a carpenter by trade. With the addition of the Harper family, the Dahlin boys, and the Petersens last week we are now thirty-two in number, but Bob Snyder not only got the stockade up and the exteriors and roofs built on the cabins but made several improvements in the camouflage. This latter is important, for I saw with my own eyes at Hadley what the skycraft will do if they see you. It is only too bad that we couldn't have saved the gray camper, for it would be as good as having another cabin. But I see that I'm straying from the story, or "narrative" as Brenda calls it.

Continuing where I left off last entry. I drove the camper away from the scene of the ambush towards Traxler, although I didn't dare go that far because I expected it also to have been in the hands of wildmen, same as Hadley. (I found out later that this was not so, and in fact Traxler was completely deserted having been netted by one of the skycraft and all the poor people taken away God knows where.) (But I did not know this at the time.) But there were five dirt roads and two paved leading to summer homes, tourist lodges and so forth, and even the old mine road could be used in a pinch.

Only a couple of miles down the road and Brenda was on her feet again insisting that she was all right. She is a remarkable woman, and I set her and the boys to watching the trees for any sign of trouble. With the wind in my face because of the smashed windshield it was hard for me to see. The pickup must have just kept going, for we never saw it again.

I decided that the old Martindale place was our best bet, which turned out to be a lucky choice.

The road leading up to it is easily missed from the highway, and I hoped that it had been overlooked by the wildmen. The turnoff was about four and a half miles this side of Traxler, and another mile or so up to the house.

But not knowing what we might find there, I stopped the camper in the trees about a quarter mile short of the house and out of sight. Then I took my rifle, leaving Duke with Brenda and the boys as a watchdog. But I had not gone a hundred feet when I heard another dog bark. It was Toby, the Martindale's golden retriever, who is a fine dog. Which had to mean that the Martindales themselves were still here since they would go nowhere without Toby.

Thus I was not surprised to see old man Martindale on the front porch with a shotgun as I approached. But I was surprised to see three other men also armed standing beside him, because the Martindales almost never had company, which I suppose accounts for poor Miss Martindale still being a spinster. She is not a spinster now of course.

I showed myself, and a minute later I was on the porch shaking hands all around. It's amazing how happy people are at such times to see somebody wearing a uniform, even a Forest Ranger uniform.

Sept. 27 I had to stop writing yesterday because the heavy rains broke down a part of the camouflage screen covering the north side of the stockade. But once again thanks to Bob Snyder we got it repaired, although it is still raining like blazes.

Which gives me time to continue this journal. I really don't feel much like writing today, but I suppose it has to be done. Brenda, being well-educated, would be much better at it and I've told her so. But she says that she once wrote a novel, but that the publishers wouldn't have it, and so she vowed never to write again. She says the experience was "too traumatic." I guess I'll just have to go on doing the best I can.

I see that I left off when we first got to the Martindale place. We all got along fine, and you'd think it would be so with everybody, there being so few people left in the world. But it isn't so and the wildmen are a constant threat. The worst part about it is that their gangs have cut us off from making contact with the other decent folks here in the National Forest, who will have a very tough time of it this winter without help.

Along with the three Martindales, there was George Waite, his son Georgie and daughter Barbara, and Butch Robertson, all from Traxler. So with the four of us that made it eleven people in all, seven adults (or maybe eight if you count Georgie Waite, who is as tall as his father). I was regarded by all as a person with authority so I immediately took charge.

There was of course no argument about what had to be done first, and we buried Brenda's late husband in the Martindale family plot which they were kind enough to donate for the occasion. Then we settled down to business.

George Waite had been in Denver on business when the skytankers first appeared. Denver was too high for the gas to reach, but he told how it had been taken over by wildmen. At the news of billions of people being exterminated, the police apparently just gave up. Many even joined the wildmen. The people tried to defend themselves, and George who is a captain in the National Guard tried to help. He barely escaped when the skycraft began netting the city.

And it was then that I first learned about netting, although not until the next day at Hadley did any of us see it up close. (Though Mr. Waite and his children and Butch Robertson are all residents of Traxler they were, fortunately for them, some distance from the town when it was netted and only saw the skycraft from a distance.) When they got back the town was deserted, as it was when Brenda and her late husband passed through it. But I knew from what I had already seen that it would not remain deserted long, for the wildmen needed food and supplies which they could only get by looting since they were almost all city bred. George said that they were in large numbers further down and seemed to have some kind of an organization under a leader.

I made a decision then which has turned out for the good. The Martindales of course wanted to stay put, and there were suggestions for moving this way or that. But I decided to return to my cabin and fortify it against attack. Had we done any of the other things we would all surely be dead by now. And though well supplied, armed, fortified, and camouflaged here I will still not feel safe until the first heavy snow hits. I wish I could do something for the decent folks camped out in the National Forest, for the snow will surely be

their death. I am determined to at least try, but I
don't know if I will succeed because of the
wildmen.

Here was my original plan. (1) Go down to
Traxler and load up with all the food and supplies
we can carry, keeping a sharp eye (the children
could help at this) for wildmen and skycraft. (2)
Take said food and supplies up the old mine road
and store same in the abandoned mine which few
but local people know about. (3) All carrying
packs, leave the valley by the old Indian trail,
which few of even the local people know about,
and which crosses the ridge not far from the mine.
This would take us ten miles out of our way, but
we would not have to risk passing near Hadley.

The others agreed with this plan (although old
Mrs. Martindale, being rather heavy, was not sure
she could climb the trail any more). It was planned
for the first thing next morning and all went well.
We left the camper and took Butch Robertson's
Chevrolet and Mr. Martindale's station wagon
down to Traxler. We approached with caution but
the town was still deserted.

The supermarket had already been pretty well
cleaned out and we finished the job. The private
homes were also a good source, for many of the
residents were food hoarders. I posted young
Mark and Barbara Waite (age 13) as lookouts for
skycraft.

We filled the vehicles and also the delivery van
from Wesley Bros. Then we formed a convoy,
which was dangerous but we had no choice. And it
was a close thing, at that. They reached the old
mine just as the skycraft appeared.

I had commandeered the sheriff's car, and had gone on ahead. We figured that our main threat would come from Hadley, so I posted myself at the bend in the road just past Slater's Motor Court, which is only a mile from town. The wildmen had been there already and it was a grisly scene. When I saw what they'd done to Betsy Slater, who was no more than twelve years old, I wanted to go into Hadley and finish off the whole lot of them. But the skycraft saved me the trouble.

My idea was to hold them off with rifle fire as long as possible, if they appeared. Then draw them away from the mine road, which I could do easily since they had no vehicle in Hadley that could keep up with the sheriff's car. Meanwhile the others would camouflage the entrance to the mine road.

So I turned the car around for a fast getaway and positioned myself on a woody rise overlooking the town. I had good binoculars and would see the first move in our direction.

It was now close to noon and the wildmen were coming out in force. Some were eating out of tin-cans, but many looked still drunk or drugged from the night before. A few toted rifles or shotguns, and I suspected that those I had chased off yesterday had reported in and were trying to organize a posse to run me down. There must have been a couple hundred people milling about the streets.

Then I noticed that some of them were pointing into the sky. I looked up, and there was the sky-craft. It was hundreds of feet long, gray-green, and kind of shimmering like mother-of-pearl. But I saw no windows or openings and it made no noise at all. It stopped right over the village square.

Some of the wildmen ran for cover, while others stood their ground and even made obscene gestures. Then somebody opened fire with a machine-gun, and several more did the same with rifles and shotguns.

A cheer went up, and it looked for a moment as if they had actually shot down part of the skycraft. A big cone section about sixty feet long broke off the tail of the mother ship and dropped like a bomb. The wildmen (and women, of which there were a goodly number) scattered in all directions. But the cone stopped about a hundred feet above the ground and just hung there like a giant shower nozzle. There were no propellers or jets and no connection with the mother ship. And no noise at all.

After a few minutes some of the wildmen began coming back into the village square. Many still hung back, but it did them no good. Without warning a shower of gray-green filaments shot downward out of the cone. They were about the thickness of a garden hose but moved as if they were alive. None escaped, for the filaments hunted down even those that tried to hide in houses or cars.

I have called this process "netting," not so much from the way the people were caught but from the way they were pulled up into the giant cone. The wildmen tried to run and dodge, but the instant one of the filaments touched them, no matter how lightly, they stopped struggling and just stood there and waited while the filament went after somebody else.

When everybody in the streets had been touched (or stung, I suppose) the filaments darted into the houses. They seemed to know exactly where the wildmen were trying to hide, and nothing could keep them out. They broke windows, ripped open car doors, and even pierced solid brick walls.

Then the filaments began drawing the wildmen (and women) into a mass below the giant cone. And they just stood there, hundreds of them, like store-window dummies while the filaments wove themselves into a net. There was not a sound as the whole crowd was drawn upwards into the cone. Then the cone shot upwards and reattached itself to the mother ship, without leaving the faintest crack where they joined. Turning eastwards, the skycraft moved slowly away like some colossal dirigible. It was still hunting.

I got back to the mine as quickly as I could, because it was no longer necessary to unload the convoy. Nor did we have to climb the old Indian trail now, but could drive right through Hadley. Mrs. Martindale was happy to hear this, for she is a heavy woman. By nightfall we had everything unloaded at the cabin and everything safely camouflaged. The wildmen have not found us yet.

Nov. 25 I see I wrote quite a stretch the last time I sat down with this journal. It is now Thanksgiving morning and I have been chased out of the house while the women under the direction of Grandma Norquist, the farmer's widow, prepare the Thanksgiving dinner. So I'll try to bring this up to date, although not much has happened of an exciting nature since my last entry.

We've only had a couple of light snows so far, but the big blizzards will be hitting any time now and then we'll be more or less snowed in until spring. But although there are now 47 of us, we are well stocked with food, firewood, supplies and so forth. I should have more time over the long winter months to keep up with this journal (although Brenda has a Great Books Discussion Group organized and has enrolled me as a charter member).

Which reminds me about the books. In going back, I see that I mentioned the loss of the camper, which to me only meant the loss of a possible place to live. But to Brenda of course it meant much more. In fact she was actually willing to risk her life to go back to the Martindale place where the camper had been left and try to rescue it (the wildmen were getting thick again in and around Traxler). She and her late husband, both being university people, had packed the camper with all kinds of important books, and had taken great pains to decide which books should survive and which should not. But to let her go back would have been letting her commit suicide, and I put my foot down. She did not argue at the time, but she sulked in the days that followed, even seeming at times more distressed over the loss of the books than over the loss of her husband.

They are calling us to dinner now so I will continue this later on.

Dec. 11 We are snowed in now since a week from last Tuesday. I meant to continue this sooner but the rescue of the Blaisdells took nearly four days, and then Brenda insisted that I read immediately one of the books for her Great Books Discussion Group. It was a rather long Russian book (translated of course) called *Crime and Punishment*, and I found it a good story, though strange. I have a week or so off while others read the book (we have three copies), and then we are all to get together and compare notes. Having little else to do in the evenings now (I of course do my share in helping finish the interiors of the cabins during the day), I have a chance to bring this up to date.

But I see that this must be confusing, since I said on one hand that we lost the books in the camper and then I turn around and say we have a Great Books Discussion Group. I suppose I should explain. It even has a funny side to it, which George Waite and I, being local people, have laughed at many times since. (Note: I was going to leave this story out since it might have been embarrassing for those concerned, but Brenda thinks it should be included for "color.") (She is much less stiff now than when we first met, which she admits herself.) It is hard to believe that so much has happened just since last May.

Anyway, as I said in the last entry, Brenda was saddened by the loss of the books. My Department manuals were no consolation to her, and she said we were now all "doomed to regress into brute barbarism." What I think she meant by this was that without books we were going to become wildmen ourselves.

As it turned out, Miss Martindale had a whole suitcase full of paperback books. But their covers all had a drawing of a beautiful young woman dressed in something loose and flimsy with a big gloomy house or castle in the background, and Brenda did not seem to think that Gothics would keep us from regressing. But when she explained what she was looking for, the answer was simple enough. (I have noticed many times that university people, while bright and with good ideas, often have trouble getting things done.)

Now the wildmen had apparently poked about Hadley sometime after we left, for next day we saw a car go up the highway, which ends eight miles up at the camp grounds. But the car came back, and about a week later I discovered that Hadley was deserted again. The bunch that got netted had pretty well cleaned out the town. But the library was not much hurt.

So the next day I posted George Waite in the watchtower where he could see the road down to Traxler (though not Hadley on account of the big hogback), and his son Georgie up on the ridge where he could relay a warning down to us. Then I drove down in the Wesley Bros. van with Brenda and her boys. Butch Robertson and Miss Martindale followed us in Mr. Martindale's station wagon.

Brenda apparently thought that the library would be filled only with more books with young women in flimsy nightgowns and gloomy old houses on the cover. But such was not the case, for the library was maintained by the State for tourists and had all the famous classics on the shelves, and all in as good a shape as the day they were first put there.

I left Brenda with her boys to stack up the books she wanted, while Butch Robertson and I split up to search the private houses for books, and also for cots and fold-up beds (the cabin was crowded now and many of us were sleeping on the floor). Miss Martindale also went looking into the houses, although not looking for anything in particular. Just nosy, is my guess.

Dec. 12 Last night Brenda read all this over and says that I "should endeavor to be more concise." Which of course means less windy. And looking it over myself I have to agree. So I'll just try and lay out the facts like this was an Accident Report. But first I think I'll finish the story about Butch Robertson and Miss Martindale (now Mrs. Robertson, as she insists we call her) because it is such a good one.

Now Loretta Martindale was long on the lookout for a husband, and was known among local unmarried men to have what is called "sharp teeth," and most (including myself) steered clear. But a few years ago she turned 40 and gave up, or so we thought. She is a heavy woman like her mother, and I have always thought her good-natured though a trifle ridiculous.

But it turned out that she was also sly and had not really given up after all. For it was really Miss Martindale, and not Butch Robertson as everybody thinks, who found the dirty books. In fact, only somebody digging deep would have found them at all (apparently they were hidden at the back of an upstairs closet), for the wildmen had occupied the house and are always on the lookout for such things.

About the books themselves, the less said the better (although George Waite, who saw them, says they were far and away the lewdest things he had ever seen, and many were expensive books printed in foreign countries). It just goes to prove again that you can never tell about people. Old Dr. Reuchel must have been close to eighty, and the nicest man you'd ever want to meet. But he had hundreds of those lewd things stashed away, and nobody ever dreamed.

But Miss Martindale found them, and immediately got hold of Butch Robertson to show him. He had already searched the house and salvaged quite a number of good books for Brenda (it was in fact Dr. Reuchel's copy of the *Crime and Punishment* book that I read), and a couple of cots used for occasional patients (Dr. Reuchel was semi-retired). In any case, Miss Martindale made sure that Butch saw the books and then left it at that, only saying of course that it was "shocking" and "disgraceful" and so forth. Which, when you think about it, was all rather sly of her. Needless to say, Butch came back to town and got the books the first chance he had and hauled them secretly to the watchtower (we often kept a watch there last summer, and it was mostly Butch who volunteered).

I didn't find this out until much later, for during most of the summer months I was on the move, collecting as many people as I could (which I regret to say has not been many due to the raids of the wildmen and the netting of the skycraft). (Which makes me wonder if this is going on all over the world and what becomes of these poor people, and of course who it is that's doing the netting.) All this time Butch had Dr. Reuchel's collection of dirty books, and apparently they did the trick for it wasn't long before he got interested in Miss Martindale which he never had been before.

But Miss Martindale insisted on being properly married, which was impossible because as far as we knew there were no clergymen, justices of the peace, sea captains and so forth left in the world. It was Brenda who saved the situation. I had salvaged a big leatherbound ledger from the lawyer's office in Hadley, intending to use it for keeping a record of supplies. But Brenda set it up as our "official register," in which all marriages, births, deaths and so forth were to be made legal by being written down in front of two witnesses.

So that is how Loretta Martindale became Mrs. Elwood Robertson. Although it is a good story which we have laughed at many times (including Brenda), it was probably a good thing for Butch, who used to clean up the bowling alley in Traxler and sometimes got into trouble on account of his drinking (which has been completely put a stop to because of his wife's firm hand with him). Brenda and I were next to put our names in the official register as being married, and we are now expecting our first child.

I never did see the dirty books (not that I'd be interested in such things) because when Grandma Norquist heard about them she gave them all short shrift. Butch had just been officially married, but was on duty one day at the watchtower where he kept the books when

Grandma Norquist, her daughter Ingrid, and Mabel Snyder, Bob's wife, marched up. They threw all of Dr. Reuchel's dirty books in a heap and put a match to them. Butch got a couple of healthy cuffs from Grandma Norquist, and so that was the end of that.

March 19 We were ready to leave at dawn, but then the blizzard hit. We can't stay here, for as soon as the snow melts the wildmen are sure to attack. For the last week I've been at it twenty hours a day. We all have, each doing what he (or she) does best. Bob Snyder made the sleds for our sick and wounded (Brenda too must go by sled since she is now eight months pregnant). It was almost by chance that I discovered that Seminoe Wells was deserted. Or, to be truthful, almost deserted. There were six wildmen there when I arrived, the old residents having apparently been netted. But with all that's happened I have become like a wildman myself. There are over a hundred men, women, and children looking to me to save them, and God as my witness I will save them. I shot those six wildmen down like dogs, and now Seminoe Wells is deserted and we must somehow get there if we are to live.

Looking back over this journal I can't believe that I'm the same fool who wrote such nonsense. I don't know if this is doing me any good. I was all keyed up to start for Seminoe Wells. It is a good 30 miles north of here. If Poison Creek was not still frozen over we wouldn't have a chance. We can follow it most of the way, but the pass will be difficult. I would not be writing this at all except

that I didn't know what to do with myself when
the blizzard hit. Brenda suggested it. I can't sleep,
though I've been up all night. She says that I
should not rip up the above nonsense, though I
certainly feel like it. She says that she will walk
and leave the sled for the children, but Grandma
Norquist told her she'd hit her with something if
she even suggested it again. And I agree, so Brenda
will take the sled.

The wildmen are organized under a leader. We
burned them out of Hadley, but they are a small
army in Traxler and have gotten a lot of snowmobiles from somewhere. Mary Madlock, who
escaped from them, says it's mostly me they're
after (especially their leader, a vicious swine who
calls himself "Billy the Great"). But from others I
have rescued over the winter I have heard terrible
tales of torture and cannibalism (I have seen signs
of this in several places). Brenda says that there
are "historical precedents" in besieged cities and
so forth. But in any case they are now determined
to get us. Last summer I avoided the wildmen, and
killed them only in self-defense. But now I hunt
them down, and shoot them on sight.

I am a hunter and a Forest Ranger, and most of
them are city bred. Were I alone I would not run,
for even though there are thousands of them they
would be no match for me in the forests and mountains. But there are the old and sick and wounded.
I must get them to Seminoe Wells somehow.
Beyond that is the canyon country where no skycraft or wildmen will ever find us. We can go there
when the snow melts. And after we've settled there
in the caves and canyons, then maybe I will come

back here and settle a score or two with these murdering savages. Especially Mr. Billy the Great.

May 27 I keep meaning to catch up on this journal, but something always gets in the way. Brenda is always encouraging me to catch up, saying that this will be a "vital document for posterity" and so forth. But when there's still skycraft to dodge, wildmen to fight (although these are now disorganized and less of a danger since I shot their leader), and food to provide for over two hundred people, then I'm afraid posterity will just have to get to the rear of the line. But it's raining again today, and having nothing else to do until we leave tomorrow morning (providing of course that the rain has stopped, I'll try to catch up a bit.

It was almost a miracle the way we got through. There was a heavy snow the day before we left, but it stopped all at once and the skies cleared. Which meant that our trail would be easy to follow. Every sheet and white piece of cloth we had was sewed into cloaks for all of us, and we had white blankets to throw over the sleds. So when the skycraft appeared we just blended into the landscape and it glided right over us. It stopped a few miles away, and the back part of it dropped down below the trees. (Later, I found out that a whole gang of wildmen were moving toward our stockade in snowmobiles and that they got netted, so it was really the skycraft that saved us.)

We reached Poison Creek in good shape, and since it was frozen solid and covered with snow it was like a perfect highway through the forest

right up to within a few miles of Seminoe Wells.
Thanks to Bob Snyder we all had good snowshoes,
and I had seen to it that everybody knew how to
use them. The dogs, however, had trouble in the
deep snow and had to be taken onto the sleds,
which they did not much like.

Butch Robertson was my head scout, having
done some hunting up here, and he was the one
who brought in the two boys (Donald Braidwood
and Harvey Kruger, ages 14 and 17), which led to
the discovery of Dr. Gustavson's party, which
were in a bad way when we found them.

There are no towns or camp grounds close to
Poison Creek on account of the sulphur in the
water, but it passes about a mile or so north of
Mineral Caves. And that's where Dr. Gustavson
had holed up with close to sixty people. But only
half of them were still alive, and few if any would
have lasted till spring.

I'll admit right here that my first thought was to
just keep on going. As I said, there were over a
hundred people to get safe to Seminoe Wells,
which by itself was touch and go. Once I got them
there and settled down, I probably would have
tried to come back and see what I could do. But
Brenda is what you call "idealistic," and would
not hear of passing this stranded party up, though
she was having a hard time of it herself. So I
settled the people for the night (at Waterpocket
Cliffs, where they could light a fire and not be seen
from above or below, though I had hoped to reach
Little Bear Gulch, which forms a kind of
crossroads to either the basin and range country
to the west or Seminoe Wells and the canyon

country to the north, before dark). Then I had the boys, Donald and Harvey, lead the way.

It took us the better part of the night, but we saved them all. One poor little girl (I regret to say I never did learn her name) died the next day, in spite of all we could do, and we turned aside to bury her in a small cave out of the reach of the wolves and coyotes. But the rest we brought through safe, and every one is with us here today. It took all our sleds to get them back from Mineral Caves, for many were too weak and sick to walk very far. And here again credit must be given to Bob Snyder, who must be accounted a genius with wood, for having built several new sleds by the time we got back.

I had hoped to make it in three days, but it took us over a week. The pass alone took two days, and we were all exhausted from pulling the sleds. Fortunately for us, Seminoe Wells had not yet been looted by the wildmen, for our food was gone when we finally reached it. That was on the evening of the seventh day.

May 28 Postponed on account of rain, like they used to say about the baseball games when there were still such things in the world. But there's no real hurry now, so we can leave tomorrow. Or the next day for that matter. Then who knows when I'll have another chance to write in this journal? So I'll bring things up to date.

Looking over yesterday's report, I'm embarrassed to see that I did not even mention the baby. It was a fine healthy boy, born the third week after we got here, and we named him Clark after the river that borders the National Forest. There have been three other babies born, and all have been duly entered in our official register, along with the two new marriages we have had.

The idea may have been mine, but the real credit must go to the women, again led by Grandma Norquist, who did the wonderful work. The white cloaks were of course no good for camouflage after the snow melted. So I wondered if some kind of cloak couldn't be made from grass and leaves and such. Well, Grandma Norquist and the other women set to work and produced such wonderful cloaks, including big hoods, all so cunningly sewn of grass and bark that you have to look twice to see somebody dressed in one at a distance of only ten feet. So when the skycraft appear we just blend into the landscape so to speak. But we still have no idea what these people who are flying the skycraft even look like (though there are of course many wild guesses), nor what becomes of the poor folks who get netted.

Now what I am about to put down has been much debated between Brenda and me. She says (often) that "revenge is the least noble of human passions," and the whole matter remains a sore spot with her. Although, I must admit, that I did and still do look at it in a different light. So I'll just lay out the bare facts, and let it go at that. When next I pick up this journal (which may not be for some time on account of us leaving tomorrow, that is if this rain ever lets up) who knows but I might not feel different about it all. So here are the facts.

After the baby was born and I saw that both he

and Brenda were doing fine, and that the folks had enough to eat and were well guarded and so forth, I decided it was time to settle a few scores. I see by looking back that I have given no real idea of the grief caused us by the hordes of wildmen. I have no time to go into all that now, maybe later I will do so. For now I'll just say that several were killed, many wounded, and some including children captured whose fate is unknown though guessed at from accounts given us by Mary Madlock, who escaped from them, and from others I rescued.

I told Butch Robertson what I was up to, in case I did not get back, but just let the others, including Brenda, who I did not want to worry, think that I was going out scouting as I often did. The snow was mostly gone, and I loaded up with food and ammunition and headed across country for Traxler.

This was not just a private feud (although in all honesty revenge for the rotten things done to us played a part), but was necessary to our safety. Of this I cannot convince Brenda, although it seems obvious to me. You see, the wildmen were dangerous mostly because they were organized. In normal times I guess that Billy the Great (as he called himself and demanded that others do like-wise) would have been just a cheap crook or public nuisance of some kind. But to give the murdering swine his due, he was a good organizer. Therefore, killing him would probably break up his thug army (it did). The wildmen are now disorganized and present no great danger to us. But Brenda still does not see the logic of it all and considers my actions "deplorable."

Traxler had been turned into an army camp, like maybe the kind Attila the Hun might have had. I got there on the third day, and was surprised at all that had been done. There were scouts and guards and maybe a thousand or more (including hundreds of women, mostly young, who were just as mean and dirty looking as the men) in Billy the Great's thug army. Though they lived in the houses and stores, these might just as well have been Stone Age caves from the looks of things.

And there were prisoners, seventy-four of them as it turned out. Fortunately, they were all kept in the Pillar of Fire Baptist Church at the east side of town, which had been turned into a prison. I was able to rescue those poor people, but I regret to say that not all of their young women and boys could be saved because the wildmen had some of them that morning, though thanks to little Karen Wheeler many were rescued.

The scouts and guards were easy to evade, for they did not know the lay of the land as I did. Arriving late in the afternoon of the third day, I got a good look around through binoculars. There was a muster, like in a regular army, and even the women fell in with the rest. It was a ragtag affair, but it was organization nonetheless. Then out strolled Billy the Great, who was apparently living in old Mrs. Sorensen's big white house right in the center of town. I had heard him described, but this was the first time I had ever seen him. He wasn't much to look at, for he was stocky, with short legs and bushy red hair and beard, and he wore thick spectacles. But there was no doubt who was boss, from the way the others jumped whenever he said anything.

But I see I've been rambling again, though I meant to just put down the bare facts. The rain is letting up, and we will be starting as soon as it's light. So I'll wrap this up for now.

When I learned of the prisoners, I decided to rescue them if I could. But I was determined to get Billy the Great too. So I laid my plans, got a couple of hours sleep, and came back after dark. Blackout conditions prevailed in Traxler, on account of possible skycraft, so there was not much risk in going right near town. There had been three scouts posted between Traxler and the old mine road, but I had taken care of these and they would never scout again. The whole thug army, including the women, were dressed in ragtag military uniforms, and I switched clothes with one of the dead scouts. Thus I was not suspected when I entered the town. Only one guard even questioned me and I made short work of him.

The Pillar of Fire Church sits on a hill. I approached from the rear, finished off the guards (four), and entered the church. Though I was dressed like the wildmen, some of the prisoners recognized me, as they had camped in the National Forest in previous years. Many were in a bad way from beatings and starvation. Some had to be carried, others had daughters and sons in the hands of the wildmen and did not want to leave.

But I got them started along the old mine road, then I returned to Traxler. I planned to wait until Billy the Great held his ragtag muster in the afternoon, and pick him off with my rifle. Then I would return to the mine and lead the prisoners over the old Indian trail, which I had told them about in

case I did not make it back, but which the wildmen
were unlikely to know of. But I got lucky, for the
bodies of the guards I had killed were found, and
this created a commotion. It was just dawn, but
the thug army was already being roused. This
meant that Billy the Great would be out soon, and
I slipped into town where I could draw a bead on
the front of old Mrs. Sorensen's house where he
lived.

I was just turning onto Franklin St. in the dim
light when I came upon another guard, a big hairy
lout with a shotgun. He had his back to me, but all
was silent here on Franklin St. I had just decided
to go up Pershing instead, when something
suddenly jumped out of the shadows near the
guard. It was a fourteen-year-old girl (I found out
Karen's age later) and she dived out of the
shadows at that guard like a lynx, swinging a
hatchet right into his face. He dropped like a sack,
but the shotgun fortunately did not go off. The girl
stared at the body for a minute, then started
hacking at it like a fury, moaning and gnashing her
teeth.

When I got close (but not too close) I saw that
she had a black eye and puffed cheek and lip.
When I called to her, she jumped up and I thought
for a second that she would come for me with the
hatchet too. But I identified myself, and named
some of the prisoners I had rescued and so forth,
and at last calmed her down enough to talk. I told
her the way to the old mine road, but she would
not go. She had a younger sister somewhere in
town, plus friends. I asked her if she thought she
could round them up without being caught, and

she said, "Yes." And she did too, thirteen of them (including her sister Kay). A brave girl, Karen Wheeler, she never once cried, neither then nor later.

I had to wait a good two hours (on the roof of Woolworth's, beneath a camouflage net) until I got a clean shot at Billy the Great. It was a head shot at less than a hundred yards and the bullet caught him just over the left eye. The wildmen (and women) had been in pretty bad shape to begin with on account of drink and drugs, and they hardly even tried to catch me (not that they ever could have anyway).

Karen Wheeler rounded up all those on this side of Traxler, but unfortunately those on the other side could not be rescued since there was no way of crossing the highway without being seen. We set fire to the rest of the town. This is what I had done earlier in Hadley, which deprived the wildmen of a place to camp.

It took us ten days to get back to Seminoe Wells, because we had to live off the land — but I got every last one of them through, and tomorrow at dawn we start for the canyon country.

CHAPTER IV:
THE LAST OF THE CARSWELLS

There was a soft tapping at the bedroom door. The Chief Snyderman and the two witnesses had arrived; all was in readiness. Thelon replaced the manuscript in the wooden chest and followed Tatoka into the main room.

He now knew that the big leather-bound ledger had merely been picked up by chance in some lawyer's office centuries ago. But he observed the ritual nonetheless. Leafing backward through nearly a century of precise entries, he wrote beneath the name George Madlock Carswell:

DEATH: October 9, 407.

The two witnesses were traditionally the two oldest able-bodied men in the stockade. They now stepped forward and stared down at the entry for the prescribed two minutes. Neither could read, but the ritual was centuries old.

Closing the ledger, Thelon nodded to the bearers. The four men dressed in hooded cloaks of bark and grass placed the body in the lichen-stained coffin; the Chief Snyderman himself sealed it. The Old Man had been Mentor since before even the two witnesses were born. Thelon followed the coffin all the way to the outer palisade.

Burials always took place at night. The grave would be dug in some secluded part of the forest, then disguised in such a way that not even the sharpest eyes would find it in the morning. Hundreds of people stood about in the dark stockade; Thelon could feel their presence. The death of the Old Man was the greatest event in living memory, but there was not a sound. Such was the ritual.

Tatoka held the blackout curtain for him. She was in better control of herself now. All that had given meaning and purpose to her life was gone, but she had done her duty to the last. She bustled about the cabin, ordering the two girls and the handyman this way and that, cleaning the already immaculate rooms.

Thelon returned to the bedroom. There were a few hasty entries in Walter Carswell's Journal, telling of a trip through some place simply called the "canyon country." Then there were no more entries for decades. The next entry was barely legible, scrawled in the stiff hand of someone long unaccustomed to writing.

Jan. 7, 41 Forget about this old journal. Brenda found it while packing up to move here to this new stockade. Bob Snyder's men done their usual fine job, though Bob himself passed away—why my God it must be twenty years now. Not many of the old bunch left. And though they all tell me different I know I'll be joining them soon. Funny though, after all I been through that it was just an ordinary cut on a rock that got me at last. Fell down and cut my knee. But this time infection set in. Guess my circulation's not so good any more. The pain is sometimes bad. First time I ever really been laid up like this, though I'm going on seventy-seven in July. But I don't think I'll make it. Brenda thought this old journal of mine would give me something to do to pass the time until I'm better. But I think she really knows that this is it for me. Fine woman, Brenda, and we wouldn't have achieved half of what we did without her. Especially about the books and learning. Probably have ended up just like the wildmen. Ideals mean a lot in the long run. I've learned that, though I didn't used to believe it.

Jan. 10, 41 Been off my head the last couple days. But I feel a little better this morning, though still weak as a kitten. Reread that old story about how sly Miss Martindale nailed Butch Robertson. That was a good one! But they are both gone now. I thought at first of going back to pick up the "narrative" as Brenda calls it but I'm not up to it. I think we're safe now, leastways we have not been bothered by skycraft for maybe 35 years since we came here. And it was just lucky that we found this place. For wherever we settled it wasn't long before the skycraft started getting thick looking for us. So we had to move on and always north. And at last we came here. Our son Clark is a wonderfully educated man and a son to be proud of. Likewise our grandson Thelon and it is fitting that one should be named for the river at the beginning of the road and the other for the river at the end. They would have been famous men for their learning if things had been different. Brenda says that they are "mentors of the people" and it is her that the credit must be given to though I am a college graduate it was only Eastern Montana A & M and I studied forestry. But it is only a guess why we are not bothered here for the skycraft never come directly overhead, though they are sometimes seen in the distance especially over the Barren Lands beyond the forest. I used to read science books and manuals put out by the Department. And when we fled from Ft. Smith we almost got lost because of the compass acting funny (pointing south when we were actually going north and so forth). But I remembered about magnetic anomalies and I am sure that this is one and it covers about a hundred square miles for I have checked. Maybe it throws off the compasses of the Hunters which is what the skycraft people are called not on account of always hunting us (leastways they did years ago) but on account of the big game animals that are not from this planet. My dog Duke, part collie and part German shepherd, was killed by one. Oh, but that was a long time ago. But I really should say something about the animals . . .

That was the end of the journal. At the bottom of
the last page, in a neat feminine hand, was added a
brief postscript:

> On the fifteenth of January in the 42nd year of
> our wanderings, Walter Patton Carswell passed
> away. His journal, though fragmentary and incom-
> plete, shall be carefully preserved for posterity. A
> beloved husband and father, a leader who, though
> he sometimes felt compelled to act with
> regrettable harshness, led, sustained and subse-
> quently protected over a thousand helpless people
> in this our northern sanctuary. His loss is
> irreparable. In the words of the immortal Bard:
> His life was gentle, and the elements
> So mix'd in him that Nature might stand up
> And say to all the world, "This was a man!"
>   Brenda Michaelson Carswell

For several minutes Thelon stared silently down
at the old manuscript. As a boy — provided that he
washed his hands first — he had sometimes been
permitted to look into the big ledger that recorded
the three major events in a person's life. Elwood
Robertson, Karen Wheeler, Anna Norquist, Bob
Snyder; their deaths were recorded one by one in
the first few pages, along with those of Walter
Patton Carswell and Brenda Michaelson Carswell.
Though he did not realize it at the time, he had
long known how the story had ended. Now he
knew how it had begun.

The newspaper clippings merely recorded the
spread of the poison cloud, speculations as to the
origin of the skytankers, and local relief measures.

There was a particularly vivid account of rioting and looting in a city called Chicago. But the clippings all seemed to be from small-town newspapers, presumably collected by someone in the Carswell party as it fled northwards. More interesting were the manuscripts in the Old Man's handwriting.

Thelon smiled at some of these: youthful sonnets, a long-abandoned diary, and even four acts of a tragedy in blank verse entitled "Dido of Carthage." At last he found the manuscript he had been looking for. But it was a disappointment. The "stranger" who had been picked up just inside the boundaries of the Anomaly generations ago may not have been a stranger after all. His name was Kruger Martindale, and his delirious ramblings sounded almost like one of the fairy tales in the Old Man's library. Flyings through the air, great shambling ogres, humanoid dogs and apes; even some prehistoric monsters.

Thelon pondered over the manuscript for nearly an hour, although it was a scant ten pages long. He had first heard of it by chance, but the Old Man had been too secretive to let it be known that somebody had once left the Anomaly and returned alive. Kruger Martindale had been captured by some wildmen, escaped them; then was driven far to the south, where he was captured again, this time by the Hunters. At least, that was the story Thelon pieced together out of the man's delirious ramblings.

It seemed fantastic. But two things made him pause and wonder. The animals described by Kruger Martindale were clearly not of this earth.

But neither were the mammoth game animals of the Barren Lands, which had surely been brought here from some other planet. There was also mention of being caught in some kind of net that stung — just like the "netting" described in Walter Carswell's Journal. Thelon returned the manuscripts to the wooden chest and locked it. He was disappointed that so few of his questions had been answered. But right now he was faced with an even greater question — survival.

Winter came quickly to this remote corner of the planet, and it was long and cruel. But thanks to Thelon's tireless activity, it soon began to look like the most bountiful harvest within memory. By using some new methods which the Old Man had always refused to let him try in the past, the gleaning and, especially, the fishing produced unprecedented yields. The norquist women were kept busy from early morning until late at night just processing what was brought in. Poaching was largely a matter of luck, but even here they were successful.

One of the mammoth game animals, fleeing the roundup out on the Barren Lands, was spotted not far from the edge of the forest. It was only a matter of time until the drover machines caught up with it, but Thelon acted quickly, organizing the largest hunting party ever known to the people. The Old Man would never have done such a thing.

It was a monster unknown to the zoology books in the library. A great shaggy brute the size of an elephant, it was shaped something like a rhinoceros, although it had a pair of five-foot horns sticking straight out of its forehead, rather than a single or double snout horn. They came upon it at twilight, as it grazed in the open brush near the boundary of the Anomaly. It was risky, but Thelon decided that the chance of getting tons of fresh meat for the winter was worth the risk. He himself led the charge out of the trees.

The brute was caught by surprise; it screamed and bellowed as a deadly rain of spears and arrows assailed it from all sides. Thelon dodged in under the terrible horns and rammed his own spear into the monster's side. Then he led the people quickly back into the safety of the trees.

They watched as the monster staggered and fell to its knees, a bloody froth oozing from its great jaws. It tried gamely to rise again, but it had been mortally wounded. The moment it crashed onto its side in its death throes, a swarm of poachers, almost invisible in the fading light, were upon it. There would be no food rationing this winter.

By the time of the first snows Thelon had made his decision. He had moved into the Mentor's cabin; Tatoka was his housekeeper. But it was important that he minimize the usual winter duties of his office. He had much to prepare, and all too little time.

The people had always managed to survive the winter, but sometimes there was hunger and rationing. The Old Man had always lived in a continual succession of rationing councils and inspections, the continual exercise of his authority; nothing so enhanced his importance as a crisis did. Thelon knew that he had secretly enjoyed the mental challenge of these problems. But this would be a winter of plenty, the most bounteous within living memory. There would be little need to call upon the Mentor for decisions.

The atlases in the library were centuries old, but it was unlikely that the physical features of the planet had changed much in so brief a period of geological time. The distribution of forests and plains was another matter. The mammoth game animals of the Barren Lands were creatures of the plain. But what other kinds of animals had the Hunters imported to the planet Earth? Creatures of the forest? The desert? The swamplands? There was only one way to find out.

Through the long winter evenings he pored over the ancient maps, memorizing the location of every significant lake, river and mountain to the south. Nor was he alone among his books. He had taken the further unprecedented step of opening the Mentor's library to the people. The few who had somehow learned to read were delighted, and made great progress. He even organized reading classes for the children. Elwood and Gustavson deeply resented this, but did not dare say anything to his face.

He also spent an hour or two each day in the target shed. He was already a formidable marksman; a few of the older men drew heavier bows, but none more accurate. In the days to come he would have to live off the land, perhaps in regions where the plants and animals were strange to him. He could not afford to miss.

His woodcraft was beyond that of any wildman. But most of all he depended upon his speed. He was by far and away the fleetest runner in the entire stockade; his tall, slender form moving with the speed of a wild animal. Even if the wildmen spotted him in the open they would stand little chance of running him down. This fleetness was to become very important indeed, in ways he could never have suspected.

But there was no defense against the Hunters except camouflage. The traditional hooded cloak of bark and grass was too cumbersome for a long journey. But what to replace it with? While browsing through the library one day, in search of some books for the children's reading class, he came upon a book that he himself had not read since childhood. And there was the answer! He took the book to the Chief Norquist Woman and opened it to the illustration of Robin Hood. In a very short time he had a warm, comfortable, skillfully made suit of motley green.

He designed and redesigned the pack he would carry, continually excluding unnecessary items. Beginning with a staggering knapsack, he ended with a small leather pouch that could be hung from his belt. Needle and thread, flint and steel, map and compass, a few small tools for shafting arrows — what else did he really need? From the other side of his belt he would hang Walter Carswell's binoculars, which had been preserved like a sacred relic for generations. He already had a good sleeping bag.

Rumors spread rapidly through the stockade. But it was not until March, when afternoon temperatures sometimes climbed above zero, that the Chief Snyderman visited him late one night. Tatoka had already washed up after supper and retired to her own room to catch up on her sewing, and Thelon opened and closed the blackout curtains himself.

The Chief Snyderman was a stocky, graying little man barely five feet tall, one of the few who could read. He had spent much of his leisure time this winter poring over Walter Carswell's now yellowed and brittle Department manuals. These had given him many new ideas. Though he followed the traditional methods of the snydermen, his mind was too practical to have become completely ritualized — as happened all too often these days. He listened silently to Thelon's plans.

"But why go alone?" he asked, concerned solely with the practical aspects of the journey.

"Because I can travel faster, cover more territory, and at less risk than if I were to take others with me."

The Chief nodded his head, appreciating the conciseness of the reply. "Yes, I see that now, Thelon. A single traveler might elude the wildmen, but a party would make it worth their while for a strong effort. Yes, I see that."

"Also, there are the skycraft."

"Yes, Thelon. And the same principle applies there."

Thelon smiled. The Chief's practical mind had grasped something which he himself had not seen before. The "netting" described in Walter Carswell's Journal was too expensive a process to be wasted on just one man. Or even a small group, for that matter. Perhaps that was why the wildmen lived only in small, scattered groups;

they were everywhere, but never in large concentrations.

Thelon carried the old wooden chest in from the bedroom. "There are documents in here that I don't want Elwood or Gustavson to see. They will both be living here while I am gone, and though the chest is locked they might be tempted to break it open. The documents will do them no good, but might do them and others serious harm. Perhaps when they are older —"

"And you want me to hold the chest until you return?"

"Keep it safe for a period of, say, five years. I should return long before then, and if I do not you must assume that I am dead. Here is the key."

"It will be as you say, and I give you my word that no one will open the chest until then. When do you leave?"

"By the end of next month."

The Chief shook his head doubtfully. "That will be dangerous, Thelon. Even in June blizzards are not unknown. But in April —"

"I have a good sleeping bag, and have often lived outside the stockade, even in winter. And I will be travelling south, where spring comes earlier. I do not plan to return to the stockade next winter, nor perhaps even the winter following. The seasons are mild where I am going, and far to the south the winters are like our summers. But I doubt if I will go that far."

"I see that you have thought much about this journey. That is well. I have always believed in careful measurement beforehand. Time is saved in the long run, and much effort as well. But what

will you tell the people, Thelon? They know the
stockade only, and are afraid of everything
beyond."

"Perhaps I should just tell them that I'm going
to look for new supplies of food and resources?
What do you think?"

He replied thoughtfully, "I agree, Thelon. You
have already used new ways in harvesting. Many
were worried at first, for such things had never
been done before. But the result proved the
method true, and this has been a winter of plenty.
That you would now go seeking even greater
resources is in keeping with this."

"Then that is what we shall do."

The Chief Snyderman carried the chest to the
door, but stopped before reaching the blackout
curtain. He turned and looked thoughtfully up at
Thelon.

"Many years ago I asked your great-grandfather
a question. But he would not give me a true
answer. It is something I have always wondered
about."

"Ask, and I will answer if I can."

"Has the world always been as it is now,
Thelon?"

"No, it was once much different. Before the
Hunters came, men once ruled the planet Earth
and their numbers were almost beyond reckoning.
Read, and you will see. Elwood and Gustavson
may not like it, but I will see to it that you and the
other readers continue to have free access to the
books while I am gone. But I see that you still have
questions."

The Chief Snyderman smiled wryly. "One

question seems to lead to another. But I have already taken enough of your time."

"If you have questions, ask. I will answer if I can."

"That is well, Thelon. But I will only ask one question now, for I know that you have much to do." He paused. "Since boyhood I have heard tales of the Hunters. But what are they really like?"

Thelon shrugged. "That is one question I cannot answer, for I do not know myself. Nor is the answer in any of the books. It is one of the reasons for my journey, to find out who these Hunters are. All I know is that they are not from this planet and that they are immensely powerful."

The Chief Snyderman nodded his head thoughtfully. "This is a great thing you are doing, Thelon."

It was not until the night before he actually left that Thelon allowed Elwood and Gustavson to move into the Mentor's cabin. They were already trying to give orders, but he saw to it that they did their own packing and hauling. Nor would old Tatoka be bullied. She had promised Thelon to look after his two pompous, absurd young cousins while he was gone, but she was already watching them narrowly for a chance to put them in their place.

Thelon had been careful not to humiliate his cousins in public; he knew how vital was the mentorial authority to the survival of the people. Nor would the people really miss him if he failed to return. Their lives were so ritualized by now, so perfectly adjusted to the environment of the Anomaly, that they might survive just as they were now for untold centuries yet.

Even the dangers of inbreeding were obviated
by taking in from time to time the youngsters of
the wildmen and Indians. Old Tatoka had come to
the Anomaly as a girl of eleven, escaping some
punishment. But the Indians were almost never
seen in the region any more; they had evidently
been surprised by a skycraft during a religious
gathering some years ago. Small bands of
wildmen still hovered about the boundaries of the
Anomaly, a continual threat.

But Thelon wanted more than mere survival,
more than a cringing, ritualized existence within
the confines of a sub-arctic sanctuary. He had no
idea what he would find outside the Anomaly,
perhaps only his own death. But he had read
books, and he knew that the earth had not always
been as it was now. He would leave just before
dawn.

It was now common knowledge that he was
going — presumably to search for new resources — but he had kept his exact date of de-
parture a secret. Only Tatoka knew. She roused
him about three hours before dawn, on the last
day of April in the 408th year of the wanderings.
He dressed quickly in his suit of motley green. He
had laid out his gear the night before. His snowshoes and rolled sleeping bag lay ready by the
door.

He let Elwood and Gustavson sleep. He had no
great hopes for their future development; the Old
Man had probably selected them for that very
reason. They would carry on the rituals of the past
unchanged, but he doubted that they would ever
have much success bullying Tatoka. The old

woman prepared his breakfast stoically, although he knew that her heart was breaking.

Only when he was donning his fur parka beside the blackout curtain did she show any emotion. She tried to press on him the sacred charm she had worn around her neck since childhood, but he would not let her. He spoke gently to her, as he had the night that the Old Man died. At last he slipped through the outer blackout curtain into the night. The curtain and the door closed behind him without a sound.

It was a clear moonlit night; the temperature was well below freezing, but there was no wind. The faint whisper of snow beneath his feet was the only sound as he crossed the stockade. Neither sound nor smoke nor the faintest glimmer of light betrayed the fact that a thousand people lived here. A solitary figure stepped out of the shadows at the gate. It was the Chief Snyderman.

Perhaps the transfer of Elwood and Gustavson to the Mentor's cabin had given his practical mind the clue. But somehow he had divined that Thelon would be leaving today. The two men removed their mittens and shook hands. There was no need for words. The Chief Snyderman was a foot shorter than Thelon and had to reach up to pat him encouragingly on the shoulder. Then Thelon slipped through the narrow entrance to the stockade.

There had been a few brief thaws in recent days, but the snow was still deep. He knelt and locked on his snowshoes. Then he turned and glided swiftly away though the dark boreal forest.

CHAPTER V: DEVIL WORSHIP

Following a map is not as easy as it looks, especially if that map is centuries old. Thelon was rather skeptical about his compass. The needle had always pointed one way inside the Anomaly; but he was only a few miles outside its boundaries when he discovered that the needle had reversed itself. He relied mostly upon his own woodcraft as he moved steadily southwards.

The snow was his great ally, turning the maze of lakes and rivers into open highways and confining the wildmen to their squalid lairs. With the exception of two days of blizzard, which he weathered beneath a rock shelter, he forged steadily ahead. It was when he ran out of snow that his real problems began. The world seemed to dissolve overnight into an endless morass of muck and flood water. Then the wildmen came out.

Sickly, wretched creatures dressed in reeking animal skins, they were far more numerous than he had anticipated. But he soon learned to avoid their caves and dugouts, and was seen and pursued only three times in over a thousand miles of travel. In each case his fleetness of foot saved him. His only real skirmish, when a band of wildmen pinned him down on the bank of a flooding river, ended victoriously. The survivors were driven howling back into the trees, but he lost several precious arrows.

For two weeks he followed the embankment of an ancient railroad almost due south. There were ruins here and there near the shores of the small lakes that checkered the landscape, but nothing that might have once been a city. With the melting of the snow the rivers became obstacles rather than highways, and they all seemed to run the wrong way. But only when he reached the big lake did he actually take to the water. It was hundreds of miles long and studded with islands; he was fairly certain that it was Lake Winnipeg.

The wildmen were everywhere now, although never in large groups. The big lake seemed his safest route south, but if the old maps were still valid it would bring him dangerously close to the open country. He was no longer worried about the skycraft; only large gatherings of human beings interested them.

He had no trouble stealing a canoe from the wildmen. There was some primitive fishing gear inside, and he put it to good use. Traveling by night and sleeping on one of the deserted islands by day, he reached the foot of the long lake without incident. But in the days that followed he had increasing difficulty finding a safe place to sleep.

The landscape was completely different now. This had been a region of cities and towns; ruins were everywhere, and ancient railroad embankments criss-crossed in all direction. There were thousands of abandoned vehicles, rusted hulks of metal. He had encountered these before; some of them had contained skeletons. But now they seemed to be everywhere, and those that had some protection from the elements were often in surprisingly good condition. Good enough, at least, to provide a safe refuge while he slept.

At first he had wondered if they really would be safe. Many showed signs of having been recently broken into; although, strangely, none of these contained human skeletons. He had left his fur parka hanging from a spruce tree hundreds of miles to the north. He still had his sleeping bag, and was confident that he could outfight or outrun any wildman living — but not while he slept. He decided at last that the rusty old vehicles were his safest refuge. Even if they tried to break in, the noise would surely wake him. That would give him at least a fighting chance.

But the strangest thing about the wildmen was that they all seemed to be moving in the same direction. It reminded him of the ancient "folk wanderings" he had read about. Their bands were the largest he had yet seen, sometimes eighty or a hundred strong; many of the bands led bound captives. They were not hunting parties, and he grew more and more curious as the days went by.

Where were they all going? And why? Surely even their dull minds realized that they were in danger from skycraft.

Then he came upon something so macabre that he had to know the reason for it. The strange migration continued to move solemnly toward the open country to the southwest. They seemed to have been caught up in some kind of religious mania, a weird pilgrimage toward some kind of primitive shrine. At the rear of the largest procession, nearly two hundred strong, he saw a mysterious black wain being drawn by chained captives. Focusing his binoculars, he saw that it was filled with human skeletons, hundreds of them. His was a journey of discovery. He determined to follow them at all costs.

It rained most of the following day, a cold, nasty drizzle that continued well into the night. But the procession of wildmen, still drawing the grisly black wain after them, continued undeterred toward the southwest.

Thelon followed in their tracks at first, but after being delayed several times by stragglers who were too sick or weary to keep up, he moved off into a parallel track. He was continually on the alert for skycraft, but none appeared.

His parallel course brought him through the outskirts of what must once have been a large city. On the far side of town he saw some rusty railroad cars; nearby stood some rusty machines that he could not identify. They hovered like giant insects over a row of unnatural conical hills.

The buildings of the city were now mostly rubble, and fires had gutted large sections. Still it seemed preferable to the squalid caves and dugouts used by the wildmen. But for some reason they made a wide detour, as if they were afraid of something. In fact, they would not even approach the ruined city until broad daylight.

Thelon cut straight through the center of town, saving several miles of travel. He was hours ahead of the procession when he sat down on a hillside to eat. He had the remains of a haunch of venison; a clear spring bubbled out of the base of the hill. It was an overcast day, but the rain had stopped.

After eating, he bathed in the spring, sitting naked in the wind until he was dry. His suit of motley green was worn and travel stained now, and he had had to make some repairs along the way; but it was still warm and comfortable.

He climbed to the top of the hill and scanned the countryside through his binoculars. The trees thinned out to the southwest, but otherwise the forest stretched unbroken as far as the eye could see. The strange procession was still a couple of miles away. He wondered how much longer it would take them to reach wherever they were going. He also wondered why he had not seen any skycraft lately.

As he swept the binoculars back toward the procession of wildmen he caught sight of a strange animal. It was a carnivore of some kind, and even from the distance of several hundred yards looked gigantic. He was sure that no earth carnivore was so huge, not even the Kodiak bears he had read about. The creature's front legs were larger than its rear, and it reminded him vaguely of a giant hyena. But its gray hair was long and silky, and it had a shaggy mane about its heavy jaws. It walked with a limp.

An ancient wall of fieldstone cut diagonally across a small clearing; the procession was moving directly toward it. The huge carnivore crouched behind the wall like some incredible cat beside a mousehole. Only when the wildmen reached the clearing did Thelon realize how cunningly the monster had positioned itself. The wildmen carrying spears were naturally in the vanguard, but the procession had to march on the opposite side of the wall from the crouching monster in order to reach an opening at the far side of the clearing. Those farther back in the procession were unarmed.

The instant the marchers reached the opening, the monster bounded over the top of the wall right into the midst of the procession, slashing right and left with its great talons. Its roar was like thunder. Five wildmen were brought down before the rest could scurry out of range.

One of those dragged down somehow got to his feet and tried to stagger away, but the monster grabbed him from behind in its huge jaws. He shrieked and writhed in terror, pleading for help. But the others made no move to rescue him, nor any of the four others who lay wounded several yards away. They seemed happy that they themselves had not been dragged down. Some even laughed.

Despite its crippled paw the gray carnivore had brought down five wildmen through stealth and cunning. The man in its jaws continued to writhe and cry for help as it settled itself comfortably on

its haunches and began to devour him. The others
circled out of range, slipping through the opening
in the wall as quickly as they could.

Two of the four wildmen stretched out on the
ground still showed signs of life; one leaned on his
elbow trying pitifully to rise. But no one made a
move to help, though hundreds passed by only a
few yards away. The gray carnivore continued its
meal.

Thelon had read of predators that turned man-
eater when crippled; lions and tigers, for instance.
This creature had somehow injured its right rear
paw, but it seemed more intelligent than any lion
or tiger. Perhaps it had come here after being
injured somewhere on the plains to the southwest.
No longer able to hunt its natural prey, it had
begun preying on the wildmen. They seemed to
recognize the creature, although it was surely not
from earth.

For two more days he trailed the procession
toward the southwest. Never had his vigilance
been so tested. Other processions of wildmen were
now converging from all directions; not only were
their scouts a constant menace, but their
increasing numbers made him more and more
nervous about skycraft. His binoculars never left
his hands the last few miles to the corrie.

It was here that the processions were
converging, a deep corrie that sat among the hills
like a natural amphitheater; it seemed from the
distance as if it might hold thousands of wildmen.
But his view was obscured by a wooded ridge
about a mile to the west. The procession he had
been trailing was apparently one of the last to

arrive. They were still threading their way through the forest when he saw his chance to slip closer to the corrie.

He circled behind a smaller procession of wildmen, keeping his eyes open for stragglers, and made it to the wooded ridge without being seen. It rose perhaps two hundred feet above him. The climb was not difficult, and the dense verdure screened him from below. He found a broad rock ledge near the crest. There were only three processions of wildmen in sight, the largest by far being the one he had been trailing. They were now converging rapidly.

An uncanny wailing suddenly arose from the other side of the ridge, but he could not move higher without exposing himself. There was a notch about thirty yards to his left, and he scrambled toward it, using the trees and underbrush for cover. The notch was evidently some kind of glacial water gap; it veered sharply back to the right and downward. He crept forward, stopping every few yards to listen. The wailing grew louder and eerier.

Then it ceased as if cut by a knife, and a blood-curdling scream rose out of the corrie. Thousands of voices roared out their response. Thelon stopped in his tracks as if struck by a blow. The notch concentrated the roar until he could actually feel his ribs vibrate. Then there was another scream and another thunderous response. They seemed to be trying to frighten him off.

But his curiosity was too great for him to turn back now. He began looking for a safe place from which to use his binoculars. A heavy feral stench rose out of the corrie, pierced by the reek of fresh blood. He saw a crack in the rock wall and crept toward it. He could see the entire west corner of this natural amphitheater. More important, he could see the altar.

The corrie was a good fifty yards across at the top and perhaps a hundred feet deep. Thousands of wildmen sat upon the slopes like the devotees of some obscene temple. Devil worship had returned to earth. Eighty or ninety bound captives stood helplessly in two rows just beneath him. The altar had been hewn from some lustrous gray-green stone, serpentine perhaps; it shimmered like the skycraft of the Hunters. Thousands of human skulls ringed the grisly amphitheater. Three of the captives had already had their throats cut. Horror and loathing overwhelmed him, and he had to turn away.

Then he saw a larger crack in the rock wall, through which he could command a view of the entire gathering. The corrie opened onto a narrow valley to the east, and at last he saw the procession he had been trailing for the last several days straggle into view. They left their hideous black wain at the mouth of the corrie and filtered silently up the slopes. The ceremony continued.

It was then that Thelon first really noticed the three costumed witchdoctors. Until now he had been more concerned with the captives. But what he had taken to be merely crude robes turned out to be very carefully made costumes, molded from some rubbery leprous-white material. All three witchdoctors moved with jerky, uncoordinated motions, evidently in imitation of something. They reminded him strangely of giant mollusks.

Nearly all the captives were wildmen — squat, hairy, wretched-looking creatures. The few women were of the same type. There were only two exceptions. One was a young man in the very front row; small and thin, his skin was even paler than the leprous white of the witchdoctors' costumes. Though it was an overcast day, he blinked and screwed up his face as if the light were too strong for him. He was dressed in patchwork garments that looked like they had been cut from a crazy quilt.

The other exception was even more striking in appearance. Tall and lithe, he had the disproportionately long legs of a cheetah or greyhound. His gray-green tunic seemed to be made of some fine leather; around his neck he wore a metallic gray-green collar. He lay on his side somewhat apart from the other captives. Thelon saw through his binoculars that his right leg had been badly slashed or bitten, and that he was weak from loss of blood.

The three witchdoctors began dragging a wailing, terrified captive toward the altar stone; one of them carried a strange broad-bladed knife. Still moving with spasmodic jerks, they bent the captive backwards across the altar stone, exposing his throat. Then the witchdoctor with the broad-bladed knife spastically raised his arm. The helpless captive shrieked in terror as the blade touched his throat. Thelon lowered his binoculars, turning away in disgust.

The next instant he was running for his life, out of the notch, down the wood ridge, and into the

forest with every ounce of his great speed. One of
the gray-green filaments shot after him like a
living spear; but he beat it into the trees. A
moment's hesitation, a stumble, and he would
surely have been netted.

Walter Carswell's Journal had described the
skycraft as moving slowly through the air, like
ancient dirigibles. The few that he himself had
seen had always moved that way. But this skycraft
had shot out of the clouds like an arrow, stopping
so fast above the corrie that it was a wonder that
everything inside had not been smashed to jelly.
The giant cone had dropped from the rear of the
mother ship like a meteor. But by then Thelon was
half way to the forest. Only when he was well out
of range did he stop and look back.

This was the closest he had ever been to a skycraft. It was hundreds of feet long, gray-green in
color, and shimmered like mother-of-pearl.
Exactly as Walter Carswell had described them.
That much at least had not changed in the intervening centuries. But this was a predator
immensely more powerful than even the gray
carnivore he had seen a few days ago.

He raised his binoculars. The wooded ridge
obscured what was happening inside the corrie.
The truncated skycraft still hovered directly
above it, silent and ominous.

Minutes passed, and still nothing. The skycraft
began to seem almost like a natural formation,
like the wooded ridge of the hills beyond. Then all
at once the giant cone appeared above the ridge; it
rose smoothly toward the mother ship. There were
no rockets or propellers of any kind; the sixty-foot

section just seemed to ascend of its own volition. There was not a sound.

The instant it rejoined the mother ship all signs of juncture immediately disappeared. Then the skycraft turned and glided slowly away toward the southwest, just beneath the dark blanket of clouds. Thelon waited until it was out of sight; then rose and crept cautiously back toward the high ridge. There was not a wildman in sight, and no sound but the faint thrumm of the forest.

But he had no idea yet how efficient the netting process was. When he again reached the notch in the wooded ridge he was even more cautious than he had been the first time. This would be a natural escape route for any wildman trying to flee the corrie.

But the ancient water gap was deserted; so too was the corrie, where only minutes ago thousands of wildmen had thronged the slopes. Only their feral stench and the reek of fresh blood remained. Even the narrow valley beyond was deserted. If any wildman had escaped that way they were still running. He angled his way down the slopes to the bottom of the corrie.

Thousands of human skulls grinned at him from posts and rock ledges; but they showed no sign of weathering, and the wood of the posts was still green. In fact, he found a pile of freshly-cut posts not far from the altar stone. There were also striations in the corrie floor, indicating that the altar stone itself had only recently been dragged into place. The black wain filled with human skeletons still stood near the mouth of the corrie. Evidently this evil ceremonial center was still under construction. Perhaps this was the first time it had ever been used.

Thelon gave one final look about the corrie. The shimmering gray-green color of the altar stone was like that of the skycraft. But what of the three witchdoctors? What devils or demons had they been trying to propitiate? He turned his back in disgust.

Whatever they were up to, he thought as he left the corrie, their magic must have been extremely potent. Never had the faithful been so quickly gathered to their just reward. He crossed the narrow valley and headed back through the forest.

It was nearly sunset before he reached the outskirts of the ruined city. He had finished the last of the venison; tomorrow he would have to hunt. The cloud cover had dissipated, and a soft breeze wafted out of the south; a few rose-golden clouds drifted across the setting sun. It would be a balmy night; but also a dark one, the moon would set barely an hour after the sun.

The gray carnivore had brought down five wildmen only yesterday; but it was of a monstrous size and voracity. Nor had he any idea what other creatures might have wandered in from the plains to the southwest. He began looking for a safe place to sleep.

In the blood-red glow of the setting sun he roamed the deserted streets of the city. The buildings had been mostly of brick and clapboard; few still stood above the second story. The single stone structure he came across had been gutted by fire; it looked ready to topple at any minute. He began looking for abandoned vehicles.

He found what had apparently been some kind of small delivery van; it sat beneath one end of a concrete viaduct, the central span of which had collapsed. The front windows were spider-webbed with cracks, rust had gnawed holes in the body, but in the windowless rear section no wildman or wild animal could get at him without waking him. Besides, it was too dark now to look for anything better.

The hard floor of the van made him think regretfully of his comfortable sleeping bag. He was tired from his long day's march, but at first sleep would not come. There were no noises of any kind to disturb him. In fact, the silence was almost eerie.

Drowsily, he recalled how the wildmen had seemed afraid to enter the ruined city, even going miles out or their way to avoid it. Which was just as well, he decided. At least no wildman would be sneaking up on him in the dark. He yawned, and tried to find a more comfortable position . . . .

And, suddenly, he was wide awake. He knew that he had been asleep. For how many minutes or hours, he could not say. But he was awake now, all his senses alert. He felt, rather than heard, the presence of something alien, something monstrously large. He listened, hardly daring to breathe.

For several minutes he heard nothing. The wind had picked up while he slept, and it soughed mournfully past the rust holes in the body of the van. Had he imagined it? Was that really the faint padding of some huge creature, or merely the wind? His palms grew moist; he felt the hair on the back of his neck rise.

The crash was sudden, stunning. The blow hit the side of the van like a sledge-hammer, sending showers of rust down from the roof. The ancient vehicle groaned and shuddered beneath the blow. The second crashing blow was even harder than the first. But the steel panel held. Then he heard the angry snuffling of some monstrous animal. It had not been his imagination.

The blows had come from the right side of the van, and the only door he had been able to open was the right front door. He had not been caught in his sleep, but he was now trapped. The ancient, rusted panels would not hold up long against the sledge-hammer blows of whatever was trying to get at him.

Through the cracks of the front windows he could see a narrow band of stars, but their light was too feeble and distant to do him any good. He could not even see what was trying to break in. There was no moon.

The next blow smashed through the paneling, and he felt a huge paw swipe at him in the darkness. He slashed at it with his hunting knife, diving out of reach and pinning himself against the left side of the van. The roar of pain and anger was thunderous; it stunned him, depriving him for a moment of the will to resist. But the huge paw was withdrawn.

Then he heard an angry snarl as the creature moved to the front of the vehicle. The tail-gate doors opened outward; but they were locked tight by centuries of corrosion. He felt for the handle, but it too was frozen with rust. Leaning against it, he felt it give slightly. He was afraid that it would

break off in his hand if he pushed any harder.
Then indeed would he be trapped.

Suddenly, a tremendous blow smashed in the
front door, and he heard the sound of falling glass.
In desperation he threw his whole weight against
the handle. It did not break, but it hardly moved at
all.

The narrow band of stars was blotted out by
something that seemed as big as the van itself. The
roar struck him like a blow, and a huge paw caved
in the front windows. Frantically he hammered at
the handle. It gave an inch or two — then snapped
off in his hand.

Whirling around, he met only black terror. The
stars were blotted out; the monster was smashing
and clawing its way through the rotted front
panels of the vehicle. Thelon felt about him for his
bow and quiver. By touch alone he nocked an
arrow and let fly into the very heart of the snarling
blackness.

The roar almost knocked the bow from his hand,
but the creature only kept coming. He fired two
more arrows point blank, but they only seemed to
make it more angry. He could see the band of stars
again, for part of the van's roof had been clawed
away. An acrid, unearthly stench filled the com-
partment.

Lying on his back facing the tail-gate, he began
to kick frantically at the rust-frozen doors. There
were no windows; it was the lock or nothing. But
the lock would not give. The creature was right
behind him now. Only its great bulk kept it from
reaching him.

Flakes of rust fell like snow, sweat poured into

his eyes; and still the lock would not yield. Then suddenly his right foot seemed to be kicking at an angle. The hinges! He jumped to his knees. The right upper hinge, nearly rusted through, had given way. Grabbing the top of the door in both hands, he wrenched it back and forth until the second hinge snapped. The door fell from his grasp. He snatched up his bow and quiver, diving through the opening just as the enormous paw slammed down behind him.

He scrambled blindly up the slope. He had to find some place too small for the huge creature to get at him. A tree? But what if it could climb? And if it had been able to track him over brick rubble and stone, it would be able to track him anywhere. It was so dark that he could only see objects when they were silhouetted against the stars.

He stumbled and nearly fell among the rubble that littered the streets. The creature was right behind him now, and he fled blindly through alleys and passageways. One fall could be his last; but caution too might be fatal. Placing one hand on a low wall, he vaulted over it; landing in thick shrubbery on the other side. He stopped and listened. The padding of heavy paws entered the alley he had just left, coming right for him. The wall would be no obstacle.

He groped his way downward through a maze of shrubs and trees. At the bottom of the slope he came upon a crumbling structure of brick. Most of the roof was gone, but the walls were still intact.

He turned around and saw a monstrous black shape silhouetted against the sky as it clawed its way over the wall. It was twelve feet long and stood higher at the shoulder than he did. As it started down the slope he saw that it limped.

He tried to slip silently into the ruins; but in the darkness he stumbled over some loose bricks. There was a roar behind him, and the great beast pounded inexorably down the slope after him. Feeling his way in the dark, he edged forward into the crumbling structure.

He came upon a staircase leading up; but two steps convinced him that the rotted planks would not hold his weight. Then he came upon a basement staircase. He did not like the idea of being trapped in the basement like a rat. But the monster was right behind him, and he knew that its senses were far keener in the dark than his own. Perhaps there would be a storeroom below, or a shed he could barricade. He had no choice.

He plunged blindly downwards, hoping the planks would hold his weight. The fetor of ancient decay engulfed him. Using his bow like a blind man's cane, he tapped his way across the slime-encrusted floor. He reached the wall just as the monster reached the top of the stairs. For a moment he hoped that the opening would be too small; but then he heard the rasp of its shaggy coat as it squeezed through the doorway.

Running his fingers along the wall, he discovered a door hanging by only one hinge. It would not stop the beast for long, but perhaps he could barricade it with something. He reached out with one foot and touched only air. It was another stairway, leading down into what had probably once been a wine-cellar. He closed the door behind him, wedging it into place; but the bolt broke off in his hand.

Tapping with his bow, he discovered a tier of

wooden casks. But they had all been staved in. He
heard an angry snuffling just outside the door. His
groping hands touched a row of empty racks;
there was broken glass underfoot. The floor
sloped downwards, seeming to follow the contour
of the hill. A strange odor rose from somewhere
just ahead. Then the door he had just wedged into
place was shattered with a single blow, and a roar
like thunder crashed through the blackness.

The monster was in the wine-cellar now; he
heard it limping slowly toward him, as if it were
now sure of its prey.

Abandoning all caution, he plunged blindly
forward. Broken glass clattered beneath his feet,
his footing gave way. He stumbled and nearly fell.
Catching himself, he grabbed some kind of shelf,
but it broke off in his hand. Something hit him on
the side of the head, and he felt himself falling. His
left arm scraped the wall; he was hit on the back
and shoulders, then the forehead. He was
unconscious when he hit the bottom.

CHAPTER VI: THE CLOWN

The first thing that Thelon noticed was the smell; an animal musk that seemed to be everywhere. But it was so dark that he was not sure at first that his eyes were really open. Then he realized that he had been listening for something above him; but for the moment he could not remember what. The silence was absolute.

Then he became aware of the pain, a sudden twinge at the side of his head. As he raised his hand to touch it, several more aches and bruises awoke all over his body. His back and shoulders were sore; his left forearm was scraped raw. But with the awakening of the pain, his other senses awoke too.

Now he remembered what he had been listening for. There was not a sound anywhere above him. But how much noise does the cat make outside a mousehole? He had no idea how far he had fallen, and he began testing for broken bones.

He seemed to be in one piece; bruised and scraped and badly shaken, but with nothing broken. That probably meant that he had not fallen very far. Surely not more than ten or fifteen feet. He sat up and shook his head.

He was still groggy, and it was several minutes before he tried to stand. He had fallen onto a heap of loose debris of some kind. Stretching out his hand he touched something cold and sharp. It was a broken bottle. Then he recalled the broken glass, the empty racks and staved-in wooden casks in the wine-cellar above. At some unknown time somebody had looted the wine-cellar — from below!

Then his hand touched his bow; it lay on the debris heap not five feet away. Near it lay his quiver. The arrows were scattered, and he began feeling about for them, replacing them one by one in his quiver. He discovered several new aches as he climbed unsteadily to his feet.

Again he listened; but the silence was still absolute. He reached upward as high as he could with his bow, half expecting to have it torn from his grasp by a huge taloned paw. But he could not reach the top of the pit, so it had to be at least thirteen or fourteen feet deep.

Groping with his hands, he made a complete circuit of the walls. He discovered a rope ladder; but it disintegrated at a tug. He would not have dared climb out of the pit, in any case. He had already witnessed the uncanny stealth and cunning of the gray carnivore. The risk that it was waiting silently in the darkness above was too great. There was a blind tunnel leading into the pit, and he entered it. The odor seemed stronger here.

His back and shoulders throbbed with pain; but the tunnel was too low for him to stand. Soon it was too low for him even to walk at a crouch, and he dropped to his hands and knees. Slowly he crept forward, fighting back a rising sense of panic. What if the tunnel were inhabited? What kind of unspeakable horror might live its entire life in utter darkness? But he did not dare turn back.

At last he heard the soft plop of water dripping into a pool. He crawled painfully toward it. The pool ran for several yards along the left side of the tunnel; he cupped a handful of water and sniffed at it. It smelled faintly of sewage, human sewage. He would have to be dying of thirst before he would drink such water. But soon he might be faced with that very problem.

Neither of his alternatives looked very promising at the moment. If he went forward, he risked being lost in the darkness. If he turned back, he risked being devoured by the gray carnivore — assuming that he could even find some way of climbing out of the pit. He decided to trace the tunnel to its source before making any kind of decision.

Sweeping his bow back and forth as he crawled forward, he came at last to a place where it swept a full 180 degrees. It was a gallery of some kind, and he could at last stand upright. He rubbed his aching back and shoulder, but there was no time to waste. He was already beginning to feel the first pangs of hunger.

He discovered that the ceiling was only about a foot over his head; but there were no obstructions to either his right or left, no matter how far he reached. The wall behind him, out of which he had just emerged, seemed unbroken. Then he started forward, tapping the floor in front of him with the end of his bow.

Before he had taken three steps the bow pinged against something metallic. Dropping to his knees, he felt something cold and narrow running parallel to the wall behind him. It was raised several inches above the floor of the tunnel, and its surface was gritty as if covered with fine sand. There seemed to be no end to it. Then his hand touched some wooden planks perpendicular to the heavy band of metal.

Minutes passed before he realized what it was. How different everything seemed to a man without the use of his eyes! He reached out and tapped with his bow. He heard the metallic ping of a second band.

They were railroad tracks. He was in the gallery of a mine. Then he recalled the huge rusty machines, the abandoned railroad cars, the row of unnatural conical hills that he had seen in the ruined city above. It had been a mining town, apparently underlain with a network of galleries and driftways.

He took a deep breath and slowly let it out. All mines have entrances, and those entrances are always on the surface.

He reached into the pouch at his side; the flint and steel were still there. And he still had his hunting knife. Kneeling, he began cutting shavings from one of the railroad ties. He had hope; soon he would have light as well.

Before long he had a small bonfire going. The dry, rotting wood was easy to cut and it burned with little smoke. He had no idea what had been mined here; but there was no trace of coal gas, only that heavy animal odor, which now seemed stronger than ever. He began searching for something he could use as a torch.

About twenty yards down the gallery he found a heap of moldering sacking. That would do for the head of the torch, and he began looking for something he could use for the pole. As he did, he repassed the low tunnel out of which he had just emerged. It had not been part of the original mine; of that he was certain. Then who had dug it? And why? Suddenly he was afraid.

What more natural refuge from the poison cloud mentioned in Walter Carswell's Journal than a mine? He had read that ancient mines had highly sophisticated ventilation systems. Could the poison gases have been filtered out somehow? Anybody down here would also have been safe from being netted by the skycraft, even after the gases had dissipated. If they had been miners, it would have been easy for them to tunnel into the larders, storerooms, and wine-cellars of the city above.

But that had been centuries ago. The food supplies of the city would long since have been exhausted. If there were still people living down here, what were they like now? Could human beings confined for hundreds of years to the dark inbred world of a mine have maintained any real semblance of humanity? What did they eat? Had he escaped the savage jaws of the gray carnivore only to fall among slimy, rat-like sub-humans, creeping about through perpetual darkness in search of strange food?

His first impulse was to dash to the fire and stamp it out. But after a moment's reflection he broke off a large chunk of wood from a rotted tie and laid it carefully across the flames. What he needed was more light, not less. He discovered a pile of short poles that may have once been signal flags, and set to work making torches.

Whatever was down here would have a great advantage in the dark, its familiar element. Light was his only hope. If the slimy rat-like subhumans of his fancy really did exist, he would have a better chance of surviving if he could see them. After centuries of confinement and inbreeding, such creatures could not be very robust. But if, like rats, they came after him in ravenous, slavering hordes . . . .

Thoughts like that would get him nowhere. The rope ladder he had discovered in the pit had disintegrated at a touch. Maybe there was really nothing down here now but his own morbid fantasies. In any case, he had to keep moving. But in which direction? The gallery floor seemed perfectly horizontal. His compass was of no use, and he had lost all sense of direction.

There had only been enough sacking for four torches. But there was still a whole stack of the short poles. Taking the least warped pole he could find, he rolled it back and forth along a smooth section of the rock floor. It seemed to roll somewhat easier to his right. Lighting the first of his torches, he followed the rusty tracks of the ancient mine railroad to his left. The hand that held the spare torches was never far from his hunting knife.

Even the smoky, sputtering light of a crude torch allowed him to cover more ground in a few minutes than he could have covered in an hour of blind groping. The mine had been well worked; there were numerous shafts, galleries, and drift-ways. Rusty drills and excavating machines lay scattered all about.

He was soon confident that the long gallery he was following did indeed angle upwards. He lit his second torch from the flickering stump of the first. The stench was even stronger now, and he knew of only one animal that smelled quite like that — man.

The long gallery ended in a partial cave-in. There was an opening near the ceiling where two fallen beams formed a kind of arch; but the beams only met at the edges, and the slightest nudge might bring the rest of the ceiling down on anyone trying to wriggle through.

He backtracked into the nearest gallery that angled upwards. By the time he lit his third torch he was certain that there were human beings of some kind down here. The droppings were recent.

Perhaps the sacking was damp, perhaps he had not wound it properly; but his third torch burned poorly, threatening to go out at every step. At last he gave up on it and lit his last torch. He did not want to be left groping in the dark again, and began looking about for new torch material. It was then that he heard the footsteps.

They were coming straight toward him from the other side of a bend in the gallery, twenty yards ahead. There was only one person, apparently wearing some kind of soft leather moccasin. The footsteps halted.

There was no point in dousing his torch; its light had been seen. He wedged it into a fissure and crept forward, his hunting knife held ready. Whoever it was, no matter how hideous or degenerate, there was only one of them. Behind him lay only a terrible death. He had to keep moving upwards, no matter what monstrosity lay in his path.

He stopped just short of the bend, listening intently. He heard the whisper of leather moccasins tiptoeing closer and closer; their wearer evidently had not heard him approach and thought he was still back where he had wedged the torch. Thelon leaped out, prepared to fight to the death. But all he met was a clown.

The young man looked like nothing so much as the illustrations of ancient circus clowns in the Old Man's library. He was dressed in a patchwork costume of odds and ends of different colored cloth sewn haphazardly together. His face was chalk white; tufts of frizzy red hair stuck up like bed springs above a pair of big floppy ears; his eyes were wide with fright, and he shook so badly that he could hardly stand. Then all at once he broke out into a weak, supplicating grin.

Thelon could not help laughing, partly in relief after hours of tension, partly at his own fantasies of slavering, rat-like degenerates. No wonder the people of the olden times had so clearly loved their circus clowns. The young man sniggered nervously, but did not really relax until Thelon had returned his hunting knife to its sheath.

Several of the young man's teeth were missing; most of the others were greenish with neglect. If he was a clown, he was certainly the world's smelliest clown. He had probably not had a bath since he was born. Had all vestiges of culture vanished from the human race? Perhaps they did not even speak the same language.

"What is your name?' he asked slowly, pronouncing each word with care.

The young man stared dumbly at him for several moments. Then he grinned weakly and shrugged. Thelon repeated the question several times. He had almost given up hope of being understood when the young man suddenly blurted out:

"Mike! Name o'Mike! Yers?"

"Thelon," he said. Then he slowly and carefully explained how he had been chased by the gray carnivore. They evidently spoke the same language, but over the centuries their respective dialects had drawn farther and farther apart. The young man's eyes slowly widened, and he shot a nervous glance down the gallery, as if he half expected the monster to come charging at them out of the darkness.

"Grendel," he said in wonder.

Thelon was startled. Grendel was the name of the monster in the story of the hero Beowulf which he had read as a boy. How apt! He looked at the young man with renewed interest. Perhaps culture and learning had survived here after all, just as it had in the Anomaly.

He questioned the young man further, but he did not seem to understand what he was talking about. Slowly it dawned on him that what he had taken for "Grendel" was nothing more than a slurred "Graydevil." That name was perhaps just as apt, but hardly evidence of cultural survival. The young man grinned in supplication, as if he sensed that he had said something disappointing. He looked very uncomfortable.

For the last several minutes he had been jiggling up and back on his heels. Thelon had taken this for mere nervousness. But then the young man darted past him, scooted by the wedged torch, and disappeared into the darkness beyond. The sounds that followed a moment later explained why the poor clown had come down this particular tunnel in the first place.

He reappeared a few minutes later, tucking his patchwork shirt into his patchwork trousers. He grinned weakly, as if to say that he could not help it.

"Wanna come wi' me, Tellon?" he asked timidly, showing that he would not at all be put out if he were refused. He shrugged apologetically.

"Lead on, Mike," said Thelon, laughing. He gave the poor clown a friendly pat on the shoulder.

He fairly skipped along at Thelon's side, like a happy pup. He stood only an inch or two over five feet tall; his weight could not have been much more than a hundred pounds. His extreme pallor made his age hard to guess. Twenty-five, perhaps. One of the bound captives at the weird ceremony of the wildmen had looked like this. But where had the other odd captive come from, the one with the long legs of a cheetah or grayhound? And what was the significance of the gray-green metal collar he wore around his neck? The poor clown at his side had nothing around his neck but a ring of dirt. A dim light appeared directly ahead.

"Army people!" Mike cried. He stopped and stared at Thelon in amazement, as if he had just remembered something important. But then he looked doubtfully at Thelon's suit of motley green. "No army tan. Graydevil got 'em. 'Cept one. Blind." Then he began to talk so fast that it sounded like just so much gobbling.

"Slow down, Mike," said Thelon. "I want to hear it all, but I can't understand you when you talk so fast."

Mike dropped his eyes, grinning apologetically. They were standing just beyond a rusty pile that may once have been some kind of drilling rig. The light was somewhat stronger here, and so was the stench. The young man tried the best he could to be intelligible.

Thelon understood most of the words — if they were not spoken too fast. What they actually meant, however, was anything but clear. Army people? He thought again of the tall, lithe captive with the disproportionately long legs. But he had been dressed in a gray-green tunic, not "army tan." And the Army people, it turned out, all wore metal tags on a thin chain around the neck; not shimmering metal collars.

About three years ago these Army people (whoever they were) had made contact with Mike's people. There had been twelve of them, armed with rifles and under the command of a "lootnen." They had made a survey of the inhabited parts of the mine and a census of its inhabitants. Then they had gone away, promising to return.

And they did return — or, at least, they had tried to. Six weeks ago, about the time that Thelon was still wandering through the boreal forests hundreds of miles to the north, a small platoon had approached the ruined city. They knew their way and were well armed. But in the intervening years, between the first contact with the Army people and this second expedition, Graydevil had appeared from out of the ocean country to the southwest. There had been seven men in the platoon; there was only one survivor — blind, his face half clawed away, but somehow still alive.

It was only now that Thelon realized how lucky he had been, coming through this region alive. The fact that the gray carnivore had spotted the procession of wildmen first probably had saved his life. And had he not fallen through the ancient looter's hole, he would surely have been caught and devoured in the wine-cellar. Graydevil was ten times the size of the hyena he somewhat resembled. But no earth predator was so cunning and voracious.

The mine people had been decimated since his appearance. Mike proudly recited the census figure recorded by the Army people three years ago: 587. But he guessed that the number today would be less than 400.

They had long maintained small flocks and herds in nearby valleys. But Graydevil tended to ignore these, attacking them only when human beings were not available. It almost seemed as if he had declared war on the entire human race. Only later, under circumstances he could not have foreseen in his wildest fantasies, did Thelon learn why this was true. He listened to the young man's rambling, stammering tale.

The situation had become desperate. Even though the wildmen, who had been troublesome for generations, were no longer seen in the district. Cut off from their herds, their storage bins and larders nearly empty, the mine people had been reduced to the brink of starvation. They never left the mine during the day, and ventured forth at night only at the dark of the moon, their traditional nights for hunting and gathering; for visiting their half-wild flocks and herds. But Graydevil had learned their ways and habits, and fewer returned with each dark of the moon.

"But you said that you have hunters," Thelon interrupted. "Why don't you kill this Graydevil?"

"Kill Graydevil?" The clown's eyes bulged like those of a fish.

"Yes, kill Graydevil. I've seen him and I know how terrible he is, but there are hundreds of you. Hunt him down!"

Mike grinned apologetically. "You talk just like Mr. Waner, Tellon. He said the same thing just after Graydevil first came, must be more'n two years since. But no hunters came back, though thirty went out. Nobody'll try it again no more. Herding or gathering, maybe sometimes. Went out myself couple months ago." He shrugged weakly. "Maybe he'll die soon and then things'll be all right again."

Thelon looked sadly down at the poor clown. The centuries of inbreeding and confinement had resulted in a genetic apathy incapable of being roused, even in the face of death. But who was this Mr. Waner? As he started to ask, he realized that they were not alone.

Two children stood watching in the shadows nearby. They were about ten years old, a boy and a girl. Both were dressed in patchwork shirts and trousers, both had chalk-white faces and frizzy red hair. The girl's hair hung in a tangled mass halfway down her back; the boy's hair stuck out in bed-spring tufts like Mike's. They huddled timidly together when Thelon looked at them.

" 'Lo, Mindy," cried Mike. "That you, Timmy? We got us a visitor here. Name o'Tellon. Why don't you say hello?"

The girl, who seemed the braver of the two, nodded and gave Thelon a timid suppliant's grin. The boy edged behind her for protection.

"Hello, Mindy," said Thelon, smiling to reassure them. "Hello, Timmy. My name is Thelon. I come from a land far to the north, near the Arctic Circle. Do you know where that is?"

The girl shook her head; the boy just stared at him with unblinking wonder. Mike too shook his head, although he had not been asked the question.

"I'd like to meet this Mr. Waner," Thelon said. It was evident by now that none of these poor clowns could help him.

Mike brightened. "You'll like him, Tellon. Everybody does, though he kind of keeps to hisself these days. Tending the poor blind Army man. But," he added with an apologetic shrug, "I don't think it'll do no good. Graydevil got him. Would you like to follow me? If you don't, just say so and I won't mind."

"Lead on, Mike," said Thelon, smiling in spite of himself.

But at their first step the boy turned and fled howling in terror down the dim gallery. The girl backed slowly away, keeping her eyes glued on Thelon. He stopped and smiled at her.

"You're not afraid, are you, Mindy? Mike's not afraid. Would you like to hold my hand? I promise I won't hurt you."

She nodded shyly, and Thelon gently took her hand (which had probably not been washed within recent memory). He gave it a fatherly squeeze. The girl timidly returned the pressure, giggled, and immediately started babbling some interminable story about losing her way in the mine when she was "jes' a littler." On and on she talked, hardly stopping for breath. He was soon to discover that talking was the chief occupation of these people.

Before he knew it he was at the head of a mob of babbling white-faced clowns. Not all of them had frizzy red hair, but all were dressed in patchwork shirts and trousers; it was like an ancient carnival. Nearly all the women were pregnant or had babies in their arms.

Mike began to strut with self-importance, giving orders (which nobody paid the least attention to) and explanations (which nobody seemed to believe). Mindy assumed a proprietary air; all shyness gone now, she held tightly to Thelon's

hand, glancing back from time to time at the
growing mob with almost comical complacency.
There must have been three hundred people in the
mob by the time they found Mr. Waner.

He was a little old man with white hair and
beard; he was dressed in the standard patchwork
costume, but somehow he seemed different. His
complexion was pale, but he had obviously once
lived in the sun. Nor did he have the supplicating
manner of the others. He looked up at Thelon with
shrewd searching eyes. Then he smiled and held
out his hand.

"George Waner," he introduced himself. His
handshake was surprisingly firm for a man his
age. Then he turned and good-naturedly shooed
away the mob as one might a gathering of idle
children.

"My quarters are just around the next bend,
Thelon. We won't be disturbed there." He added
dryly, "I'd say we have a few things to talk about."

CHAPTER VII: BENEATH THE CITY

Thelon told his story without reserve. He told of the stockade in the dark forests far to the north: of the ways of the people, of their history and the things he had learned from Walter Carswell's Journal. George Waner listened intently, nodding from time to time.

The room was clean and comfortable; there was ample furniture, including a desk. Velvet curtains covered the rock walls on three sides, the fourth held a large bookcase. The old man did not interrupt Thelon until he mentioned the magnetic anomaly.

"Say! That might be the reason!" he cried. "We were always puzzled about that." Then a sad, far-away look came into his eyes. "But that was a long time ago. Must be half a century since I first stumbled on this place, one jump ahead of the savages — or *wildmen,* as you call 'em. But finish your story."

Thelon continued; but despite the old man's assurances they were disturbed again and again. Every few minutes a young girl popped in the doorway, sometimes two and three at a time. They asked the old man if they could do anything for him, but each looked curiously at Thelon. At least twenty girls appeared before he had finished his story; they all wore necklaces of old coins, their only jewelry.

The old man chuckled. "If you're looking for company, Thelon, just smile at one of 'em. They're none too clean, but you get used to that." There was a sly twinkle in his eye.

But when Thelon asked about the present situation the old man could only sigh and shake his head.

"I done what I could, these last fifty years. Made the food supply more dependable, doctored 'em the best I could, and even cleaned up the place a bit and improved the ventilation. Regular sty when I first came here! Then this Graydevil appeared on the scene, and, to tell you the truth, we're in a bad way. These poor silly people are as helpless as rabbits. The only thing that's saved 'em over the years is the fact that they also breed like rabbits." He shrugged. "Breed and babble, that's their whole life."

"But Mike said that you organized a hunting party to go after this Graydevil."

The old man tugged fretfully at his beard. "I thought it was for the best. Didn't see what else we could do. But I'd never seen Graydevil, and thought he was just some kind of giant bear. Not one of the hunters came back." He squinted at Thelon for a moment. "Here, this won't do!"

Picking up a candle, he examined the bruise on the side of Thelon's head. Then he examined his scraped forearm.

"Better get that shirt off," he said. "Can't see five feet in front of me any more." He shook his head. "But I still know a thing or two about doctoring. Now let's have a look at that scrape . . . ."

Thelon stripped to the waist. He knew about the scrape on his forearm; he now learned that he had also been cut on the back. While the old man was washing and disinfecting the wounds, another young girl appeared in the doorway.

He pointed to Thelon's torn shirt. "Take that and have it sewed, Tana. No new patches, just sewed up where it's torn. That's a good girl!"

She clutched the garment to her breast, smiled at Thelon with decayed, mossy teeth; then darted away in triumph.

The old man carefully closed the iodine bottle. "Not much of that left. Cleaned out the Compton hospitals and drug stores just after I came here. But it's mostly all gone now."

"Compton?" Thelon took out his map and opened it.

"No problem getting to Compton from here," said Waner. "You just go straight up."

Thelon found it on the map. He was even farther to the southwest than he had thought. The old vegetation maps had shown this as open country, but the forest had recaptured some of its lost territory during the intervening centuries.

Waner squinted over Thelon's shoulder for a
moment; then shuffled over to his desk and began
rummaging through the drawers. He returned
with a large magnifying glass. Spreading the map
on the table, he held the candle in one hand and
the magnifying glass in the other.

"Good detail," he muttered. "Better map than
any I've got. Yes, there's Compton all right. And
Lake Superior. Range country's right about there.
Ah, there's Mountain Iron. Better map than that
poor Army fellow's."

"Mike told me about him," said Thelon.

"He's not a pretty sight. Face is half gone, and
now there's gangrene where Graydevil chewed
away his arm. He can't last much longer. In fact,
it's a miracle he's still alive. I'll just look in on him
for a moment, and then we'll have a bite to eat. Be
right back."

Thelon rose and stretched, testing his bandages.
For the next few minutes he browsed curiously
over Waner's books. There were a few familiar
classics of fiction, but most of them were popular
thrillers and detective stories, many with ragged
paper covers and brownish brittle pages.

Meanwhile a young girl entered the room and
began setting the table. She brought with her a
musky odor that was strangely sexual; every
minute or two she glanced at Thelon. He
recognized her as one of the girls who had popped
into the room to ask the old man if there was
anything she could do for him. Without thinking,
he smiled at her.

She immediately stopped what she was doing,
dropped her eyes, and stood waiting for him to
approach. Too late he remembered what old

Waner had said about just smiling at one of 'em. All he had really meant was polite recognition, and now . . . .

"Well, well," said the old man, shuffling into the room. "So that's the way it is, eh, Nell? Ask you to bring us a bite to eat, and all you can do is flirt with our guest. Hurry up, now. We have things to talk about. Here's your shirt, Thelon. Looks like a pretty good job, too."

The workmanship could not compare with that of the norquist women, but it was evident that somebody had at least tried to do a good job. He slipped the warm, comfortable shirt of motley green over his head, careful not to pull open his bandages. The girl finished setting the table, looked back at him in a way that showed she had not just been flirting, and skipped out the door.

It was a simple meal: bread, cheese, and a fermented drink that Thelon did not recognize. It was a dark, heavy brew; but not unpleasant tasting.

"Mead," explained Waner. "That's what they used to call it, leastways. Got the recipe from an old book. Honey's plentiful hereabouts, and it's a whole lot better than seeing them drink foul water like they used to before I came here. Wish I could offer you something better. But Graydevil's put us on short rations."

"He'll have to be hunted down," said Thelon decisively. "As far as I can see, you have no choice."

"Oh, I see that all right," said Warner, shaking his head. "But try getting these poor rabbits to believe you. Especially after what happened the first time. If they think about it at all, they just hope Graydevil will die or go away. But he sounds mighty healthy to me, and too smart to give up a good thing."

"He's smart all right," said Thelon. "Perhaps the most cunning predator on earth. But he's not healthy." And he explained about Graydevil's crippled paw.

Waner said thoughtfully, "Might be able to outrun him for a short space. A few have. At least long enough to pop down a hole. But look how he tracked you through the city at night, and now with the dark of the moon —"

"I'll go after him alone," said Thelon. "Just give me a day or two to get my bearings and rest up a bit. I have weapons and I know how to use them."

"Sounds like pure suicide to me."

Thelon said, "I'd rather go down fighting in the open than cower in a hole until I starve to death."

"You've got a point there," Waner conceded. "But you'd better wait until after the dark of the moon. Maybe with a little light to see by —"

"Men also live in the sunlight, Mr. Waner," said Thelon. "When I hunt Graydevil, I'll hunt him by day." And he described the daylight attack on the procession of wildmen.

"You do what you have to do, Thelon," he said after a moment. "I'm not the one to give advice about such things any more, not after sending those poor rabbits to their death. Been down here too long." He sighed wearily. "Can it really be fifty years since I came here? The hours pass slowly, but the days are so much alike that time is hard to judge. And you're right, men also live in the sunlight. At least, they used to."

"You've heard my story," said Thelon. "I'd be

interested in hearing yours."

"Not really that much to tell," said the old man.

A small community had survived in an iron mine in what had once been upper Minnesota. They had maintained a certain standard of civilization, but had suffered from the depredations of the wildmen. These had increased in number, and the young George Waner had been sent for help to a nearby community. While he was gone his people had been overrun. The wildmen had pursued him, but by a lucky chance he had found his way here.

"Like you with your magnetic anomaly, we noticed that the spaceships always avoided the iron fields. Never connected it with a compass, though." He added, "Not much has happened these last fifty years. And, as I said, not really much of a story."

But there had been one part of the story that had caused Thelon to catch his breath. Other than a couple of first-aid manuals, he had not seen a single book on any of the sciences on the shelves. Old Waner evidently had no idea of earth's normal fauna; neither Graydevil nor the creatures he had seen in his flight from the wildmen had seemed at all alien to him. But Thelon knew better. Kruger Martindale had rambled deliriously about creatures like prehistoric monsters. Perhaps they had not been a delusion after all.

"What did these giant reptiles look like?" he asked.

"Only saw one of 'em," Waner admitted. "But that was plenty. I cut across the swamp country south of here, with a pack of savages on my trail. The thing I saw was a good thirty feet high, and walked on two legs; had an enormous tail and arms not much bigger than a man's."

Thelon questioned him intently for over an hour, until the old man began to yawn. Then he began to yawn himself. Only now did he realize how badly he needed sleep.

"Take the couch if you like," Waner said. "I see by the clock it's almost day. Time to turn in." He yawned again. "Sometimes hard to tell down here." His sleeping chamber lay behind the velvet curtain near his desk.

Thelon pulled off his boots the moment he was gone. He stretched out on the couch with his hands behind his head, wondering about the significance of all he had heard . . . .

When he awoke, the chamber was silent and deserted. A single candle, shaded and guttering, burned feebly on a shelf in the far corner. He sat up and rubbed his eyes; then he rose and stretched the sleep from his limbs. The clock on the shelf told him that he had slept soundly indeed. Waner's sleeping chamber was empty.

Then he noticed that an odd assortment of articles had been laid out on the desk. He recognized a compass and a crude map, apparently traced onto plain paper from some model. He took the candle down from the shelf, removed its shade and snuffed it.

The compass was similar to his own. He compared the tracing with his own map; the route ended (or began) somewhere in the western Ozark Plateau. There were several small metal cylinders, which he guessed were bullets; an embossed insignia patch with two stripes, which he believed indicated a corporal in military rank; a well-worn metal fork, but no knife of any kind. On a metal chain hung three oblong metal tags; their inscriptions had been nearly worn smooth by what must have been at least several generations of constant wear. Holding the top tag to the candle, Thelon read: "Bensinger, Lowell," below which was a row of numbers, the letter "A" and what may have been the word "Protestant." It meant nothing to him, and he started to examine the other tags.

"Ah, you're up," George Waner cried, shuffling through the door. "You were sleeping so sound I didn't want to wake you. An old man don't need much sleep. I see you've found Corporal Sutton's things. Died a few hours ago," he shook his head. "Probably a blessing. Graydevil didn't leave much of him, and the poor lad was often in pain. Only survivor of seven."

He continued, "But you must be hungry, Thelon. I'll send somebody in with your breakfast. I've already eaten. Just looked in to see how you were. Busy night ahead of us," he muttered, turning and shuffling back out the door. "Busy night."

A pan of clear water had been laid out for him on the table, and he washed as best he could. This time he was careful not to smile at the girl who brought his breakfast; merely nodding politely as she set the table.

Bread, cheese, and mead; apparently the standard fare. He had been forced to leave his pack behind in the rusty van when Graydevil attacked, but it had contained little he might have added to this simple meal. In fact, he had planned to go hunting that very day.

And so I shall, he thought as he drained his cup of mead.

He found George Waner in a large gallery with

some thirty or forty of the mine people. The old man looked upset. Preparations had been made for some kind of expedition — empty baskets, animal traps, milk pails, and assorted weapons lay scattered about. But the people still hung back.

"Moon's down, and they won't go," grumbled the old man. "Takes days to get 'em organized for even the simplest task, and now they want to wait till tomorrow night."

"Why tomorrow?" asked Thelon.

"First night of the dark of the moon. But they usually start a night or two before, when the moon sets real early. Got everything ready, and now they won't go."

"Perhaps they should wait until tomorrow night," Thelon suggested. "In the meantime there's the expedition of my own that we talked about." He had thought that this was a settled matter, and the old man's reaction startled him.

"Please don't do it, Thelon," he pleaded. "Hundreds of our people have been killed already. And now all the Army people are dead too, though they were armed with guns." He added in a whisper, more to himself than Thelon, "It's been so long since I've had anybody to talk to."

"It has to be done, Mr. Waner," said Thelon firmly. "You know I have no choice."

He nodded reluctantly. "You're right, of course. Maybe I've been living among these poor rabbits so long that I've begun to think like them. How do you plan to go about it?"

"First, I'll have to know the safest way out of the mine. Second, I'd like all the information you have on Graydevil's habits, hunting grounds, and so forth."

All at once Thelon found himself surrounded by a babbling patchwork mob. They had apparently been eavesdropping, and now that somebody else was going forth to face Graydevil they were all valiant with advice. They all talked at once, but only a few really had anything to say. All had heard Graydevil's name, some had even had narrow escapes; but they only left the safety of the mine during the dark of the moon, and nobody really knew what he looked like.

Waner at last managed to shoo them away. All Thelon had gathered was a vague outline of the monster's habits. It raided even the most distant cattle pounds, so its territory probably covered a good hundred square miles. But mostly it prowled the ruined city, especially during the dark of the moon. It seemed to know that that was when the people came out.

"Graydevil got in here a couple of years ago," said Waner, as he led the way down a narrow drift-way. "Killed eleven people, and all we could do about it was seal up the shaft. Safest way in and out is the old bank building. You noticed the coin necklaces some of the girls wear? Well, that's where they probably came from originally. There's a tunnel dug right up to the vault."

They climbed steadily along a broad gallery with parallel lines of rusty track down the center. The accumulations of filth were incredible. Whatever cleanliness and order there existed anywhere in the mine seemed to vary with proximity to the old man's chambers.

Carrying a small lantern before him, Waner led the way up a steep tunnel, obviously not an original part of the mine. But the tunnel did not open directly into the bank vault itself, which was made of thick concrete and steel. It veered sharply to the right and opened a few feet away. The steel door hung open; there were three skeletons sprawled on the floor inside.

"Nothing in there worth seeing, Thelon," said Waner. "Come along and I'll show you why this is the safest way in or out of the mine."

The lantern light illuminated a desolate gallery strewn with rubble. Its low ceiling was supported by rows of marble pillars, its floor was crowded with desks, counters, glass cages, and rusty office machines. But it looked more like some hideous charnel house than a bank. Hundreds of people must have tried to escape the poison cloud by fleeing to the bank vault, possibly after failing to gain entrance to the mine. They were still here.

"Watch your step, Thelon. Don't know when this old place is going to collapse. See all those barred windows? Well, they let you see out on three sides for a considerable distance, and if you go up to the next floor you can see out the fourth side. That way you can at least get out in the open without being pounced on by Graydevil. It's at the exits that he does most of his killing."

"He won't get me that way," said Thelon. "I should be able to see far enough in daylight to get a good start on him."

His binoculars would have given him an even better view. But they were probably lying smashed to pieces, in the back of the rusty van where he had almost been smashed to pieces himself.

CHAPTER VIII:
THE HUNTING OF GRAYDEVIL

It was just dawn when Thelon returned to the bank building. The scene appeared even more ghastly in the weird light filtering through the barred windows. It had rained during the night, but the red-violet clouds of morning were already tearing themselves to pieces; shafts of golden sunlight poured down on the ruined city. It was a beautiful spring morning, clean and fresh and deadly. Somewhere outside waited the most cunning and voracious predator ever to walk the earth.

Moving from window to window, he scanned the ruins on three sides of the building. There was no sign of Graydevil; but that did not mean that he was not there.

There was a better view on the second floor. But the third floor stairway was blocked with debris

where part of the roof had collapsed. Through the
corner of a barred window he noticed a kind of
stairway of heavy metal bars fastened to the
outside of the building. There was a rusty steel
door opening onto it, and after several minutes of
kicking he managed to open it far enough to
squeeze through.

The top floor was a shambles. Bird droppings
coated everything like a thick carpet; a mad flutter
of tiny wings greeted his appearance. There was
not much left of the roof beyond a skeleton framework of beams; but this was the tallest structure
in Compton, giving him a clear view in all directions.

Whether it was the noise he had made kicking
open the door, or the commotion of the birds, he
did not know. But something had attracted Graydevil. On the western edge of the ruined city, less
than a mile away, he saw the monster lumbering
toward him. It was difficult to judge its speed.

He knew himself to be a fast and tireless runner,
beyond anyone he had ever met, either in the
Anomaly or among the wildmen of the forests. But
this was a terrible beast of prey; even with a
crippled paw it had had no trouble feeding itself.
Then, too, his object was not merely to run away
from Graydevil.

The metal stairway descended to within ten feet
of the ground. He dropped to the pavement and
turned with swift strides toward the east. That
was the direction of the collapsed viaduct,
beneath which sat the rusty van; it would serve as
his hunting platform. Graydevil, he knew, would
quickly pick up his tracks — but that was exactly

what he wanted.

By some miracle his binoculars were still intact, and he hung them from his belt. He even recovered some of his lost arrows. But the van itself had been literally torn to pieces; the savagery that could rend steel like so much paper was terrifying. Thelon never lied to himself. He was afraid and he knew it; more frightened than he had ever been in his life. He ran toward the collapsed end of the viaduct.

The viaduct had evidently been built to span the city's railroad yards. The concrete rubble of the collapsed central span rose to within twenty feet of the level upper pavement; but it was much too far away to be reached by Graydevil. The metal ladder was near the edge of the collapsed section, some three hundred feet from the entrance onto the viaduct; it was a good fifty feet to the top. Thelon wiped his moist hands on his shirt and grasped the bottom rung. His knees felt almost too weak to climb, but he knew that Graydevil was not far behind. It had been much easier to work out his plans in the safety of the mine.

He was panting for breath by the time he reached the top; but there was no time to rest. Careful not to silhouette himself against the sky, he stepped across a fallen support and hurried along the cracked and weathered pavement until he guessed that the van was directly below him. But when he peeked out he discovered that he had overshot the mark by nearly ten yards, and he crept back along the pavement on hands and knees.

Even with binoculars and the perspective of the

viaduct, it was several minutes before he spotted Graydevil. The monster was now stalking his spoor, moving silently through the ruins of an ancient factory. The sight was unnerving, and Thelon drew back his head; once more he wiped his moist hands on his shirt.

The sun was well above the horizon now; the clouds were rapidly dissipating. He wished that his own fears would dissipate as quickly. Forcing himself to breathe slowly and regularly, he tried to reassure himself by reviewing his position.

The monster could not climb the metal ladder. It could only get at him by circling all the way around to the viaduct entrance; in which case he could simply climb back down the ladder. Not even Graydevil could survive a fifty-foot drop, and he would have to circle back again. This dodge could be repeated until he had put enough arrows in the monster to bring it down, he hoped. He concentrated on steadying his hands for the vital first shot.

Cautiously he peeked out over the edge of the bridge. The monster was creeping up on the van, this time from the rear. Its stealth and cunning were beyond any earth creature. Thelon nocked an arrow.

Graydevil pounced on the van with a quickness that was almost incredible in so huge a creature. He was nearly as big as the van itself! But the van was empty, and he began sniffing about for the spoor. Thelon let fly. The arrow caught the monster square in the shoulder; its scream of rage was thunderous. For a moment Thelon was too stunned even to nock a second arrow. But his aim

was better this time; though he had to lean
perilously out into space to shoot under the
viaduct. The arrow caught Graydevil in the throat;
despite the fact that he was twisting angrily about
as he searched for his attacker.

Thelon tried to duck back; but the monster
spotted him. Its yellow eyes glittered with malice;
they were frighteningly intelligent. Sizing up the
situation at a glance, it whirled about and
bounded up the stony slope toward the viaduct
entrance.

Thelon retreated up the pavement, stationing
himself beside the ladder. He nocked another
arrow and waited. Graydevil lurched out onto the
bridge, and the span shook beneath his thundering
weight as he charged; his crippled paw seemed
hardly to slow him down at all. Thelon was not
sure that he could outdistance the monster if it
caught him out in the open — a thing which he had
no intention of letting it do.

His plan was to wait until the last possible
instant before firing; then to swing himself over
the side of the bridge and descend the ladder. The
monster would then have to circle all the way back
to the end of the bridge. Meanwhile he would
simply reascend the ladder. His quiver was nearly
full, and he was a first-rate marksman; it was only
a matter of time until he hit some vital spot. But
he had underestimated Graydevil.

Just as the monster came within range, it
suddenly began dodging from side to side with
hardly any loss of speed. Startled, Thelon loosed
his arrow too soon, missing his target entirely.
Graydevil was nearly upon him when he dove

over the side of the bridge, nearly slipping from the rungs and plunging to his death fifty feet below. Death, that is, if he were lucky.

Half way down the ladder he saw the enormous hyena-like head glaring maliciously down at him. But the instant he touched the ground and nocked an arrow the head disappeared. For several moments there was only silence. Then he heard a heavy scraping sound that he did not understand. Was the span collapsing under Graydevil's weight? He ran back several yards; then crossed under the span to the other side. But still he could see nothing. The scraping sound continued.

On the ground near the van were traces of purplish red blood; he had wounded the monster, but had not slowed it down. This time he would be ready for the dodging maneuver when it charged. One good shot was all he really —

He leaped back instinctively. The whole viaduct was collapsing! The next thing he knew the huge beast was skidding and sliding down the debris heap from the collapsed central span. By the time he understood what he happened he had been cut off from the ladder. Graydevil had pushed the fallen stanchion from the top of the viaduct across to the debris heap and used it as a bridge! Could this unearthly horror really be that intelligent? Thelon did not wait to find out.

The race was on, but after fifty yards he saw that he had again been cut off. It was as if the monster had analyzed his entire plan! He veered away from the entrance to the viaduct and raced with all his great speed back toward the streets of the ruined city. With a snarl of triumph, Graydevil raced after him. Could he outdistance the crippled monster? The answers to that question were life or death.

For a hundred yards the great thudding paws were right behind him, until at last he began to pull away. But he did not dare glance back until he had reached the end of the ancient railroad yards. Graydevil was just out of effective bowshot; he had adopted the loping gait of a timber wolf, which brings down its prey more by endurance than speed. The monster's strategy was now to keep him moving until he was exhausted, then . . . .

But Thelon accepted the challenge. The monster's persistence could not be explained by mere voracity; not even by the fact that he had wounded it. For reasons unknown, Graydevil had declared war on the entire human race. Hour after hour his easy, loping gait kept Thelon on the move, too close to allow him to rest but too far for effective bowshot. The shadows of afternoon soon darkened the broken pavement; but to stumble was to die. Somehow Thelon kept moving.

The thing that saved him was the monster's own cunning. Time and again it cut him off from the bank building by feints and charges, even allowing him to get far enough away so that he could rest for a moment. It used these same tactics in other parts of the city as well, and at last Thelon realized that it was cutting him off from other entrances to the mine which he himself actually knew nothing about. This gave him a chance to eat and drink, sometimes even to sit down for a few minutes.

But always the monster kept coming. Twice

Thelon set himself for a bowshot, but the instant the monster came into range it began dodging back and forth; both arrows missed. When the first shadows of evening began to fall he knew that the chase was almost over, one way or another. In the dark of the moon neither speed nor endurance would be the deciding factor.

It was a desperate gamble, but he had to do something soon; somehow he had to get at least one good shot at the monster. He had badly misjudged its intelligence, using Earth as the measure of all things. He was already lightheaded from fatigue, his legs felt leaden; soon he would begin to stumble from exhaustion. Even now he wondered if he could scale an eight-foot wall.

He had been down this same desolate street twice before. The blind alley had been bricked off by a wall about eight feet high. Graydevil would have no trouble scaling it, but he would have no way of seeing what was on the other side. Thelon hoped it would give him at least a chance for a mortal shot, with a reasonable chance of escaping afterwards should he fail. The fact that he had been down this street before would confuse his spoor. Graydevil would not be dodging back and forth when he tried to pick it up again.

He passed the blind alley, slowing down to an easy dog-trot. Graydevil, who was just entering the street, also slowed down. Thelon jogged around the entire block, until he was once more at the corner of the desolate street. But the instant he turned the corner, momentarily out of sight, he dashed with all the strength he had left for the blind alley. He reached it before Graydevil turned the corner.

And it was lucky that the monster was not hot on his trail; for it took him three tries to scale the wall. He lay panting and trembling with exhaustion on the rubble heap that reached nearly to its top on the far side.

The lengthening shadows warned him that this might be his last chance. In the dark, in his present exhausted state, he stood no chance at all. If he did not kill Graydevil before nightfall, he himself would never see dawn. The great red ball of the sun hovered just above the horizon.

He waited until he heard the snuffling sound; Graydevil had traced his spoor into the blind alley. He nocked an arrow and silently crouched behind the bricks. The snuffling grew louder. Cautiously he peered over the top of the wall. Graydevil spotted him just as he was drawing back the string.

Thelon steeled himself for the roar, the stunning, will-sapping roar that left the intended victim momentarily helpless. But it still hit him like a clap of thunder, almost causing him to lose his balance. He recovered just in time to let fly.

The arrow flew straight through the monster's open jaws, lodging itself at the back of its throat. Graydevil reared up on his hind legs, screaming with rage and pain, clawing at his face until he had torn out the arrow. His maw was slavered with a purplish-red froth. Thelon braced himself for an escape. But, suddenly, with a last thundering scream, the monster dropped and lay still.

For several moments Thelon could only stare in astonishment. He had slain the monster! Graydevil was dead! Exhausted as he was, he felt like shouting, like calling the hundreds of poor clowns up out of their noisome tunnels and telling them they were free. The terror that walked by night was no more. He climbed onto the top of the wall, exultant in spite of his weariness, and started to drop into the alley below.

But then he hesitated, perhaps warned by some primordial instinct. He noticed that Graydevil had fallen in such a way that no vital spot was exposed. Was this mere coincidence? Was the monster really dead? Could a single arrow in the throat really have brought it down so fast? It was too dark in the alley to detect any signs of breathing. He tossed a couple of pebbles; then a brick. The monster did not stir.

There was one sure way to find out. No vital spot was exposed, but the crippled rear paw lay in plain view, its great talons curved upward like sabers. Thelon nocked an arrow and let fly. The next instant he was running for his life.

With a thunderous roar Graydevil had sprung straight at him with a quickness that had almost caught him unawares. The cunning brute had only been shamming, trying to lure him down into the blind alley. Had he jumped down from that wall he would never have climbed up it again. But the monster was now badly crippled, less able to keep up with him than before.

Thelon drew his bow and waited for it to come hobbling into range. But Graydevil veered behind the brush growing out of the steps of an ancient church; then he stopped and waited, his yellow eyes glittering in the shadows with a light of their own. Thelon could not get a clean shot, nor did he dare move much closer. He was faster than the crippled monster, but only by perhaps five yards in fifty. And if it were only shamming again . . . .

It could no longer cut him off from the old bank building; but if he now returned to the safety of the mine he might never get another chance. What if the monster recovered from its wounds? Its war against the human race would become more deadly than ever, and it would never again allow itself to be hunted by day. To hunt Graydevil at night would be suicide.

But it was getting dark fast, and Thelon dared not stay in the streets much longer. As he turned and headed toward the old bank building he stumbled and nearly fell. Out of the corner of his eye he noticed Graydevil start forward as if bracing himself for a charge. The unearthly brute had not yet given up. And if he had really fallen and injured himself . . . .

Thelon glanced up the street. There were few places in which to hide along the broad boulevard leading to the old bank building. Somehow he had to lure Graydevil out into the open for a clean shot, and it looked like the only way he could do that was to get him to charge. More than one could play at the shamming game.

Once more he stumbled; but this time he fell sprawling to the pavement. He climbed painfully to his feet, nursing his left ankle. Graydevil was some fifty yards behind him and to his left, screened by a crumbling wall. Thelon turned and hobbled frantically toward the bank building, as if he had an injured leg.

With a roar of triumph Graydevil charged out of the shadows. Thelon hobbled out onto the broad boulevard. The monster was nearly on top of him when suddenly he whirled around and sent an arrow winging straight into its yellow eye. Leaping aside, he nocked another arrow. The monster was in the open now; blinded, crippled, but still dangerous. The fifth arrow brought it down at last.

Before it could rise Thelon dived at it from its blind side and rammed his hunting knife upwards under the base of its skull. Then he staggered back, reeling with exhaustion. Had the monster reared up for one last swipe at him, he would not have escaped. But this time Graydevil was not shamming.

What happened next was like something out of a dream. He may even have fainted from sheer exhaustion. But the next thing he knew he was in the midst of a shouting, singing carnival throng. The tunnels of the mine were ablaze with light; patchwork costumes danced about him like a mad kaleidoscope; young girls tugged pleadingly at his sleeves. Then he seemed to be drinking something. He never remembered how he got to the couch in old Waner's sleeping quarters . . . .

CHAPTER IX:
THE ROOM WITH THE VIOLET LIGHT

"These people would do anything for you, Thelon," said George Waner. "You could be their king, and they'd serve you all their days."

Thelon said, "I began my journey in search of knowledge, not power. Man once walked beneath the open sky without fear. But centuries have passed, and we don't even know what these Hunters look like. I must go on."

The old man tugged fretfully at his beard. "I suppose you're right. If you were the type to stay put you never would have left your Anomaly in the first place." He shrugged. "And you might reach the Army people, at that. Who would have believed that anybody could kill Graydevil single-handed? Oh, that reminds me." He shuffled across to his desk. "This might interest you. They dug it out of Graydevil's paw. Must have been what crippled him."

It looked like an icepick snapped off at the handle; six inches long and made from some kind of shimmering gray-green metal. Thelon examined it carefully.

"It must be some kind of missile," he decided. "Nobody could get close enough to Graydevil to use it as a knife. Certainly not on his rear paw —"

"Ah, there you are, girls," cried the old man. "Thought we'd never eat."

The two girls carried a heavy tray to the table and began setting out what was to be Thelon's last meal here. It was now three nights since he had killed Graydevil, and the fare had improved with each meal. There were still the old standbys of bread, cheese and mead; but now, in addition, the girls laid out steaming platters of fish and meat, a roast fowl, and brimful dishes of berries with thick cream.

Thelon was careful not to smile at the girls, merely nodding politely. They were as docile as rabbits, but his only feeling toward these pale, sickly little creatures was pity. In any case, they would not be alone for long. The dark of the moon was a time of orgy in the world above for these people; it had been going on for the last three nights. The two girls were probably even now on their way to the nearest tunnel to the surface.

"It's just beyond the big lake that you come to the swamp country," said George Waner as they finished eating. "That's where I saw the giant reptile. Once past there and you can take the big river you were talking about. That is, if you can find something to keep you afloat."

"I'll manage." Thelon rose from the table and

began tying up the knapsack given him by the old man. Corporal Sutton's effects swelled his belt pouch almost to capacity.

"Would you like to see Graydevil's pelt before you go?" asked the old man like a child trying to put off the inevitable. "It's not far out of the way. These people are good at skinning, and Graydevil had fine, silky fur. Pelt must be fifteen feet long."

"I've seen enough of Graydevil," said Thelon. "It's almost dawn and I have to get moving. You've done a lot for me already, and I'm grateful."

"Wish I could do more." The old man shrugged. "But don't take any chances. When the Army people were here three years ago they said they'd been having trouble with wildmen, and even with the Aliens. Hunters, as you call 'em. Come back if you can, Thelon. And good luck." His handshake was firm and encouraging.

It was just dawn as they emerged into the old bank building. Patchwork figures were everywhere, straggling homeward through the gray light with filled baskets or merely strolling hand in hand. Some of them started to weep as they saw Thelon leaving; but all he could do was wave farewell and hurry southward. By the time the sun rose he had left the ruined city of Compton far behind.

Following the course of an ancient road, he marched steadily onward all that day. There were no wildmen to worry about for many miles around, thanks to Graydevil. The character of the forest was changing: there were more and more deciduous trees mixed with the conifers, more and more streams and ponds, and the animal life was increasingly plentiful.

The drainage was poor in this region, and for the next four days he came upon an increasing number of bogs and small lakes. But few wildmen. Despite the fact that he had to make a number of detours, he made good time. It was not until the morning of the fifth day that he came to the barrage.

It was over two miles long, a good forty feet high, and reinforced every hundred yards or so by colossal stanchions of shimmering gray-green metal. Its weathered condition indicated that it had stood here for centuries. But why had it been built? All it seemed to do was disrupt the region's normal drainage.

It took him an hour to find a way to the top. His ancient map indicated that the northern swamplands did not begin until many days' march to the south. But here was a swampland far vaster than anything on his map. Was that the reason for the barrage? He scanned the landscape through his binoculars.

There was some high ground about two miles to the east, perhaps a string of ancient glacial formations. All around it spread swampland — reed-choked sloughs and morasses, sluggish watercourses lined with swamp oak and hickory, and countless islands and hummocks — stretching desolately to the horizon. Flights of water birds skimmed down out of the cloudless sky; the drone of insects throbbed on the light breeze wafting out of the south. In the distance he heard the cry of some large creature he could not identify. The earth must have looked much like this millions of years ago. But this was all artificial, created for reasons unknown by constructing a series of cyclopean barrages across the natural drainage.

Then he noticed something glistening above the swamp trees far to the southeast. Adjusting his binoculars, he saw that it was some kind of gray-green metal structure, covering perhaps half a square mile. It reminded him of descriptions he had heard of the corrals of the Hunters out on the Barren Lands, which he had never actually seen. He decided to see this structure with his own eyes, whatever it was. For surely it was nothing of this earth.

Scattered shrubs and thickets covered the high ground, but none dense enough to conceal a lurking enemy. By late afternoon the wind had veered, and white fluffy clouds skudded out of the west. The spoor was increasingly ominous; these footprints and droppings were from no earth creature that he knew of. There were no wildmen to fear, and he had learned from experience that the skycraft did not consider a lone human being worth their while. But still the training of a lifetime was strong, and he glanced into the sky every few minutes.

Several times he came upon the footprints of some monstrous animal; three-toed, a yard across, and so deep that it must have weighed several tons. Then he surprised a creature that might have resembled a salamander except that it was the size of a pony. He drew his bow and braced himself for its charge. But the strange lizard merely stared at him for a moment; then waddled away into the brush. It had five toes, not three.

The sun was halfway down the sky when he finally came within sight of the large gray-green structure. It was several stories high; but he could not see windows of any kind. A small stream flowed near its outer wall; the gray-green metal bridge spanning it looked capable of supporting enormous weights.

He watched for over an hour from a small coppice less than a hundred yards away. But there was neither sound nor movement, not even a bird. And this was strange, for a flock of long-legged water birds bobbed and stalked about in a tributary stream to his right. But the stream fronting the structure was absolutely deserted; nor would any of the birds approach it.

Another flock of water birds dropped out of the late-afternoon sky, landing in the midst of the first flock. The newcomers milled about, squabbling and jabbing with their curved bills until they had established themselves.

Then one of them, evidently a stranger to the territory, saw better pickings in the deserted stream. But it no sooner waded past the limit of the flock than it suddenly leapt back as if stung, crying out and wildly flapping its wings. The other birds merely stared at it, as if to say, "I told you so." It had probably run into some kind of electrified fence.

The Hunters had surely built this vast shimmering metal structure; it did not seem high enough to house one of their skycraft, unless it extended far underground. Were there any Hunters present? They had never been seen near the corrals out on the Barren Lands; just their weird dover machines. Was this structure also run by machines?

He decided to get a closer look. It might even provide a refuge for the night. He had not forgotten the giant three-toed footprints.

He reached the bridge unhindered; but there was no sign of any kind of electrified fence. Deciding that he had been wrong, he started warily across the bridge. The next moment he was writhing with pain; he gasped for breath and tried desperately to focus his eyes; there was a wild ringing in his ears.

The shock was like being stung from all sides by countless invisible needles; although it left no wounds. Curious, he stretched out his hand — and instantly jerked it back again. There was a charged barrier here after all, an invisible "sting-fence" of some kind. No wonder the stream was deserted.

But Thelon did not retreat. It was almost dusk; the slanting rays of the sun lent his bronzed skin and beard a reddish cast. In the distance, but closer now, he again heard the cry of some unknown animal.

Apparently the sting-fence did not set off any kind of alarm, or it would have done so when the bird struck it. Nor did it seem confined to ground level; there were no birds or even insects in the vicinity of the building.

He knew that the corrals out on the Barren Lands were deserted during the summer hunting season. At least, so the poachers had always reported them. Was this structure a similar

corral? Was the sting-fence merely to protect it
while not in use? And why was the bridge so
heavily reinforced? Then a new thought struck
him.

Very slowly he stretched out his hand. The
invisible needles stung him, but this time not so
hard. Then he reared back and threw a punch. His
fist was thrown back at him and he was nearly
sent sprawling. The repulsive force was evidently
proportional to the applied force. Had he tried to
run across the bridge instead of walking, he might
have been killed.

Then he turned sideways and very slowly leaned
into the invisible barrier. His whole right side
exploded with pain, but he continued to lean
forward. It was a test of will power. His right arm
was numb; the right side of his face seemed to be
on fire; blue flashes of light lashed at his brain,
sapping his will. He drew back as if somebody else
had made the decision.

Perhaps he might have succeeded if he had had a
stronger incentive than just to sneak into a
deserted corral. There was nothing to do now but
retreat.

It was almost dark when he returned to the
coppice. This was no country to be wandering
about in at night, and he began looking for a tree.
But the only big trees he could see were separated
from him by treacherous bogs and watercourses;
so he had to settle for a fifty-foot red maple.

Climbing to the highest bough that would hold
his weight, some thirty feet off the ground, he
wound a stout cord around the trunk and fastened
it to his belt. He knew that sleeping in a tree really

meant a night of cold and discomfort broken only
by a few fitful dozes. But at least he would not be
caught in the open by something big and hungry.
Perhaps tomorrow he would get a few decent
hours of sleep.

The hours passed slowly; he dozed a few times,
but could find no comfortable position. By the
time the quarter moon rose he was already stiff
and sore. Nor did the screams and cries of this
strange swampland help his slumbers. But dawn
was only a few hours away now. He folded his
arms and once more fell into a fitful doze.

The next thing he knew he was scrambling
wildly at the bough to keep himself from falling.
The cord tied to his belt had saved him; but he had
made a lot of noise. Moonlight slanted through a
gap in the foliage, leaving him exposed. Then he
saw a black shape moving right for him. It was a
good thirty feet high and walked on two legs with
a curious strutting motion. Its great jaws could
reach him on any bough that would support his
weight. Not all the arrows in his quiver would stop
such a monster.

He untied himself and scrambled to the ground
in seconds. Then all at once he saw the pony-size
salamander scuttling in terror toward the
swamps. The monster had only been chasing its
natural prey! But it saw him now.

He crouched behind the treetrunk, ready to run
for his life the instant he saw an opening. But the
monster thundered right past him; he was too
insignificant to bother with. The giant salamander
was a much more tempting meal. But what if its
meal escaped? It might then be willing to settle for

a snack. Thelon threw his knapsack over his shoulders and trotted toward a grove of trees in the opposite direction.

At that instant he spotted a smaller reptile of the same type bearing down on him. Jackal-like, it had evidently been trailing the giant reptile in hopes of getting some of the leavings. But now it saw a chance for fresh meat. Thelon tossed aside his knapsack and ran for his life.

The reptile's curious strutting gait belied its great speed. Thelon soon realized that this was one race he would not win; nor was there anywhere to hide. The huge gray-green structure lay dead ahead, faintly luminescent in the dark. It was his only chance. Life and death were now a matter of will power. He raced for the bridge.

Groping frantically with his hands, he touched the sting-fence and was knocked backwards, both hands ringing with pain. Every instinct goaded him to haste. But he steeled his will, and slowly leaned forward. The whole front of his body exploded with pain, blue flashes of light shot through his brain. Slowly, now! Slowly! He could neither see nor hear. The pain was maddening. His whole being told him to retreat, but to retreat was to die.

Then he was through. The pain was gone, and he staggered forward, weak and trembling, his body soaked with perspiration.

There was a cry right behind him, but muffled as if it came from a long distance. He whirled around, flinching instinctively. The monster lunged at him, but it never closed its jaws. The next instant it was battling some invisible attacker that bit and stung from all sides; it screamed in pain and anger. Then it leaned back on its huge tail and delivered a tremendous kick with its legs.

The reptile weighed several tons; its kick would have knocked down an elephant. But it was thrown backwards from the sting-fence as easily as the wading bird had been that afternoon. Still screaming and kicking, it fell onto its side. It was up in an instant, using its great tail as a lever; but it had had enough of the sting-fence. It turned and strutted off through the darkness. Perhaps there would still be a few scraps left from the giant salamander.

Thelon wandered along the base of the wall for some time without finding an entrance. The luminescent gray-green walls were metal, but strangely warm and slippery to touch. He moved around to the south side of the building.

The opening was little more than a slit. But it seemed to run along the entire length of the building, about ten feet above the ground. He might have overlooked it entirely if he had not heard the restless hissing sound from inside. Backing up a few yards, he ran headlong at the wall and leaped. It was like trying to climb wet porcelain; but at last he pulled himself into the narrow opening.

All sounds beyond the sting-fence were muffled and distorted as in a thick fog. But he could now hear a medley of strange sounds from inside the structure. There was a large animal pen directly below him, with a water trough to one side and an array of nozzles protruding from the far wall; it was remarkably clean. The two-legged reptile in it was about nine feet high; it paced restlessly back and forth as if waiting for something.

Animal pens seemed to run the entire length of the building, extending well below ground level; but a network of ramps and belts just beyond the pens blocked his view into the interior. The luminescence of the strange metal made everything seem weird and uncanny; it was the only light.

He could fit easily through the two portals near the floor of the inside wall. In fact, they seemed almost to have been designed to admit human beings into the pen. But it was a good twenty-foot drop to the floor, and then he would somehow have to get past the half-grown nightmare prowling about below. He decided to see what was in the other pens.

Straddling the low opening, he pulled himself along for about a hundred feet: five animal pens, five nine-foot reptiles. The opening stretched on and on before him until it was lost in the darkness. It began to look like his only way into the building was through one of the pens.

Two pens back, the nightmarish occupant had been asleep, squatting on its great haunches right beneath the opening. But what if the portals on the far side of the pen had recessed doors of some kind? Even if he did not wake the monster by leaping past it and sprinting across the pen, there would be no way of climbing back out again. But he could see no other way into the building. How he was going to get out again, he would worry about later.

Sliding as far as possible from the sleeping reptile, he lowered himself from the opening. It was still a twelve-foot drop, and he stumbled and fell as he hit the floor. Leaping to his feet, he ran and dived for the nearest portal. There was no recessed door. The huge reptile had not stirred.

He found himself on a narrow conveyor belt, studded its entire length with thin posts surmounted by torc-like clamps about the circumference of a man's waist. The posts were spaced exactly as far apart as the openings into the pens. But the conveyor belt was still, and the clamps were empty.

The light was too dim to see very far into the immense recesses of the building. Broad ramps led in all directions; the building seemed to extend farther underground than it did above. Restless animal cries reverberated all about him; there were no other sounds. But he sensed great forces at work, watchful, unsleeping forces that would resent an intruder. The structure was apparently self-maintaining; but he knew that he was intruding here.

He followed the conveyor belt for some distance, until he became aware of a violet light directly ahead. It poured through the opening in the wall out of which the conveyor belt itself emerged; the opening was about the size of a man.

Curious, he peered inside. The light was intensely vivid, painful to the eyes; and he had to squint. But no nightmare could surpass for sheer horror the scene that met his eyes. It was like nothing so much as one of those strange illustrations in the Old Man's library by somebody named Hieronymus Bosch.

The large room was filled with silent machines, whole batteries of belts, pulleys, and mechanical arms. A wide tube ran from floor to ceiling at the very center of the room, from which extended long-fingered mechanical hands like the tentacles of a metal octopus. The thin posts that studded the conveyor-belt continued into the room with the violet light; but here the torc-like clamps were all filled. Thelon turned away in horror.

Clamped fast about their waists were rows of man-sized lizards and salamanders, half-grown bears and deer, and a frog-like creature he had never seen before. Mixed indiscriminately with these, like so many vermin, were scores of naked human beings, men and women.

Were these the poor wretches that had been netted at the devil-worship ceremony? The human race evidently meant no more to the Hunters than fodder for next season's game animals. If nothing else he had at least found the answer to a question that Walter Carswell had died without learning — the fate of those netted by the skycraft. Later he was to discover that this was only part of the answer.

As he entered the room the weird violet light struck him like a physical force. He had to squint through half-closed eyelashes as he approached the nearest human being. The man's arm was still warm! These poor wretches were still alive! He shook the man, wondering if there was some way to wake him . . . .

He staggered against the soft, slimy body of a salamander, barely keeping himself from falling. He had nearly passed out. His mind reeled and his arms and legs suddenly felt numb; he could hardly control them. Staggering like a drunken man, he turned and lurched blindly toward the opening. He could now see the ghastly light even through closed eyelids. A few seconds more and he himself would have been reptile fodder.

His head cleared quickly the moment he was beyond the range of the violet light. There was nothing he could do for the poor wretches inside the room. He had barely saved himself. The problem facing him now was somehow to escape this unearthly chamber of horrors.

For the next hour he wandered up and back in the vicinity of the conveyor-belt, peering up and down ramps, examining the strange machines and devices. He knew the general principles of physics and electricity; but most of what he saw meant nothing to him. He felt like Daniel Defoe's Friday suddenly turned loose in the twentieth century's most advanced museum of science and industry.

It was not until dawn that he discovered a way out. In the dim light now filtering through the opening above the animal pens he noticed a huge sling, apparently used for hauling the monsters in and out of the pens. He could reach it from the ramp just above, and easily climb across to the slit opening. With his escape route assured he grew bolder.

He decided to explore the level he was on before trying the ramps. It would be easy to get lost in this vast, complex structure. The feeling of being an intruder, of being watched by some resentful power, grew stronger and stronger the farther he moved from the vicinity of the animal pens.

He heard a faint chirring sound coming from somewhere just ahead. Then, as if some kind of signal had been given, the hum of machines coming to life arose from several directions at once. He could not identify either sound, but the hum of the machines seemed to be getting closer.

Behind a network of tubes and belts he discovered the source of the chirring noises. Dozens of knee-high reptile chicks prattled about the floor of an incubator. They were so hideous that they seemed almost cute. He wondered how long it would take them to grow into the kind of thirty-foot behemoth he had seen last night. Perhaps decades, perhaps only a few . . . .

The hair rose on the back of his neck and he whirled around. He had sensed something behind him. But at first he could not believe his eyes. It looked like a giant face gliding toward him out of the darkness. Ten feet high and painted with hideous eyes and teeth, it was coming right for him with four mechanical arms outstretched. It was a drover machine! He turned and fled.

Giant faces were now gliding down the ramps after him from all sides, and he knew that they would keep after him until he was rounded up. His next stop would surely be the room with the violet light. To the drover machines he was just an escaped animal.

He dodged and sprinted, making for the animal pens as fast as he could. He reached the ramp only a few strides ahead of the drover machines. Grabbing the near end of the sling, he crossed the pen hand over hand. An angry bellow sounded beneath him, but he did not look down. He was nearly across when the sling suddenly started to move, carrying him away from the opening. He leaped blindly through space.

He scrambled through the opening and dropped to the ground outside; then groped his way outward from the wall, until a jolt of pain that half spun him around told him he had reached the sting-fence. Withstanding the pain was somewhat easier this time.

At last he was through the sting-fence; he stood panting and trembling on the other side. There was a marsh not fifty yards away, and these particular machines did not look capable of taking to the water. But something rounded up the giant reptiles at the end of each hunting season. He waited to see what would happen next. But the drover machines stopped just inside the sting-fence, a row of hideous glaring faces.

They seemed to watch him as he started the long trip back to pick up his knapsack and weapons. There was none of the monstrous reptiles within sight. But not two miles away, screened from the north by the gray-green metal structure itself, the morning light revealed what looked like the ruins of an ancient village.

CHAPTER X: BRENDA

Diamonds? Were these red stones actually rubies? These green ones emeralds? Rain spattered against the windows of the ancient jewelry store, crusted with centuries of grime; thunder rumbled in the distance. It was a stout brick building with a tile roof. The looters must have died at the same time as everybody else, or they would surely have broken in here. But the cases of precious stones all about him lay untouched, and it provided a safe place to sleep.

The opaque windows blinked dimly with each flash of lightning; but the rain was beginning to slacken. It finally stopped late in the afternoon, and he left the jewelry store. The dark masses of clouds, like a giant's anvil, were now moving slowly eastward, and the sun was beginning to break through.

The village had sat on the slopes of a low hill before the general inundation caused by the barrages of the Hunters; the western half of the village was now largely under water. But this had always been a lake district, and many of the residents had owned boats.

Most of these were badly decayed; the machines attached to the rear of them were frozen with rust. He found an aluminum rowboat in fair condition; but he would have had to row with his back turned. And this was one region where he wanted to see exactly where he was going, at all times.

Some large animal had devastated the village supermarket long ago; but a few of the other shops had survived intact. It was in one of these that he found the canoe. He had been lured inside by the sight of the fishing and hunting gear. Much of the stock had apparently been equipment for various sports and games (there were a number of large black balls with three holes drilled in them whose use he could not even guess). The arrows he could always use; but his own bow had been crafted by the Chief Snyderman himself, and was far superior to anything in the shop. A few of the guns had been protected by glass cases and still functioned; but only about one bullet in eight actually fired; too unreliable. It was beneath some collapsed shelves at the back of the shop that he found the canoe.

He spent the rest of the afternoon clearing away the rubble and hauling the canoe down to the water's edge. The fishing tackle in sealed plastic boxes was like new. He fished and swam among the flooded ruins until the rain started again.

He ate his fish dinner just after sunset,

surrounded by a small fortune in jewelry. Then he compared Corporal Sutton's tracing with his own map. As far as he could determine, he could reach the land of the Army people almost entirely by water; there would be three portages and a final cross-country trek of about fifty miles. But he had a long distance to go, and there was no way of knowing how much of the old map was still valid. The cries of the great reptiles sounded through the darkness outside. He decided to do his travelling by day.

Two days of steady paddling brought him to the heart of the vast swampland. The great carnivorous reptiles tended to stick to the higher ground; but he had learned that they were aquatic as well, and he was always on guard.

Toward evening of the first day he had seen one of the big salamanders fleeing from a thirty-foot monster. The salamander won the race to the river, but the monster kept coming, using its great tail to propel itself through the water like some enormous crocodile. It caught the salamander from behind, crushing out its life between rows of savage, nine-inch teeth. Then it swam leisurely back to shore with its prey.

There would be no escape from the great reptiles once they saw him; he could neither outrun nor outswim them, and there were no sting-fences here. But their great height and the general flatness of the land allowed them to be seen at some distance. Thelon remained continually on the alert. There were more trees now; although no real forests.

The region must have been fairly populous

before the coming of the Hunters; ruins poked here and there above the desolate stretches of swampland. These provided refuges at night.

Fish and small game were plentiful. Unfortunately so were the great reptiles, and several times each day he was forced to take cover among the drowned ruins or behind one of the numerous small islands. It was the afternoon of the fifth day after his escape from the drover machines that he saw the skycraft.

It appeared suddenly out of the southwest, coming right for him. Had his breaking into the gray-green structure set off some kind of alarm after all? Had he become so much of a nuisance that his capture was now worth their while? He paddled hurriedly for the cover of a low hummock.

But the skycraft stopped above the high ground less than a mile to the east, and the giant cone dropped from the mother ship as it had when the devil worshippers were netted. But what was there to net here? Curious, now that he knew the Hunters were not after him, he paddled for shore.

Leaving the canoe hidden among the reeds, he worked his way inland through a dense grove of swamp oaks. From the branches of a high tree he had a clear view through his binoculars. But what he saw made no sense at all.

This cone section was much larger than the one he had seen before, and it rested squarely on the ground. He counted twenty-seven human beings milling about its base. They were all lithe and slender, with the same long legs of the captive he had seen at the weird ceremony. All were dressed

in gray-green leather tunics and wore identical
metal collars. There was a lissome awkwardness
about them, as if, like cats, they were more
comfortable running than walking. Most of them
were women. They seemed to be waiting for something.

Then out of the portal behind them appeared
three tugging, sweating gangs of human beings of
an entirely different type. They looked more like
hairless gorillas than men; although they too wore
gray-green leather tunics. As if specially bred for
the task, they positioned three colossal machines
about five yards apart in a row in front of the skycraft. Then they turned and shambled back
through the open portal.

Several minutes passed, and those milling about
the base of the cone acted increasingly nervous
and high-strung. Then three more figures emerged
from the portal; but these were nearly three times
the size of a human being. They were dressed in
heavy suits of some rubbery leprous-white
material; they wore heavy gloves and elaborate
headgear with visors, as if they did not want the
sun to touch any part of their bodies. Their
movements were jerky and spasmodic.

They positioned themselves, each by one of the
colossal machines. Then a throbbing alarm
sounded, and the whole pack of humans darted
away at an amazing speed. They seemed to be
coming right for him, and his first impulse was to
flee. But he knew that he was again just being
overweening; perhaps an inherent characteristic
of the entire human race. The fleet human beings
continued to race toward him like a pack of
hounds.

Then he heard the scream of the giant reptile; it had been concealed in the trees to his left. But at the sight of the hunting pack (he did not know what else to call them), the thirty-foot monster charged into the open. The pack did not even break stride, and it looked like they were racing straight for their deaths.

But the instant they reached the monster they formed a running, dodging, leaping circle about it. They drew thin daggers from their belts, like the fragment dug out of Graydevil's paw, and darted in and out, jabbing at the giant reptile whenever they saw an opening. The monster lunged at them with its great jaws, lashed out wickedly with its tail, kicked at them with its huge taloned feet; but still they continued to dodge and jab and leap.

But what was the purpose of it all? They could only annoy the monster with their feeble weapons, and no matter how agile they were it was only a matter of time until they were picked off one by one. Then Thelon realized that the giant reptile was being skillfully lured farther and farther out into the open, toward a barren rise about a hundred yards away.

One of the hunting pack was brought down; then another. The monster's kick was its most devastating weapon. Like the smaller reptile that had crashed into the sting-fence, it would suddenly lean back on its great tail and kick with incredible speed and power. Both the young women brought down had been kicked; both killed instantly.

But slowly and skillfully the giant reptile was worked toward the barren rise. A third girl, then a fourth, was brought down; both by savage kicks.

The instant the monster had been positioned on
the top of the rise, the hunting pack spread out.
They continued to run and dodge and leap, but in a
wider circle, as if merely trying to hold the
monster in place. It still lunged at them.

Then a throbbing wail arose from the direction
of the skycraft. The hunting pack instantly turned
and raced down the slopes in an ever-widening
circle. The giant reptile had time for only two or
three strides in pursuit; but that was enough.
Something exploded over the very center of the
rise like the crack of lightning, and a rain of
filaments shot down out of the sky. But the
monster had moved just far enough to avoid a
direct hit.

It screamed and bit and kicked as the filaments
writhed about its huge tail like living things. But
then they went dead, and the throbbing wail arose
once more from the direction of the skycraft; this
time at a slightly different pitch. The hunting pack
instantly closed in again. Two more women and
what may have been a young man were brought
down before the monster was repositioned at the
top of the rise.

Once more there arose the throbbing wail; once
more the pack turned and fled. Thelon raised his
binoculars just in time to see one of the Hunters
turn spasmodically and work some kind of control
on the strange machine at its side. This time the
rain of filaments was nearly on target, wrapping
themselves around the monster's right leg like a
hundred writhing snakes.

The filaments bit into its flesh; it screamed and
fought furiously, lunging and snapping and

tearing with a power and savagery that literally shook the earth. But then it began to hobble, and another rain of filaments exploded directly over its back. It was still more than a match for a whole herd of elephants. But the filaments were now falling thick and fast.

At last it stumbled and fell into a thundering heap, completely encased in a writhing network. As it struggled to rise it suddenly stiffened, as if hit by some tremendous shock, and lay still. The great reptile was dead.

Thelon slipped down out of the tree and crouched in the underbrush at the edge of the grove. The hunting pack was now milling restlessly about, more nervous and high-strung than ever. They seemed irritable, now that the hunt was over, and more than one of them had glanced in his direction. He thought he could beat them back to his canoe if they spotted him; but not if he first had to climb down from a tree. They were less than a hundred yards away.

Those killed during the chase were left lying where they fell, ignored by the living. Through his binoculars he watched the huge machines being manhandled back into the skycraft cone by gangs of stolid gorillamen. The Hunters had already climbed back inside, like ancient skindivers rising out of the hostile environment of the sea.

Then an angry squabbling caused him to turn again toward the hunting pack. Two women stood shouting and menacing in front of a slender, fair-haired girl. She watched them expressionlessly; but she kept one hand on her dagger, and her two tormentors were careful not to come too close.

Then a third, who may have been a young man, joined in the squabble, and all three began angrily berating the fair-haired girl.

Thelon was soon fairly certain that what they were shouting was not a language at all, just animal noises. But the fair-haired girl did not seem at all put out by her assailants. She stood like some silent statue of a goddess, stirring only when one of the three made a move to sneak behind her. Then a throbbing wail sent them all scurrying back to their places in the hunting pack.

The portal of the skycraft cone had closed, and a gang of perhaps thirty gorilla-men now came shabbling across the high ground toward the dead monster. They carried an odd assortment of spools, metal beams, and rollers. Then the skycraft cone rose into the air and began moving in the same direction. Thelon crept back into the trees, where he could not be seen from above.

Once more the squabbling broke out among the hunting pack. This time the whole pack seemed to be shouting at the fair-haired girl. She ignored them as if they did not exist, provoking them into a fury. She was easily the most beautiful girl of the entire hunting pack; but why they were angry with her, Thelon had no idea. The skycraft cone was nearly overhead when the girl's two original tormentors attacked her.

The girl drew her dagger and calmly awaited the onslaught. Instantly, a throbbing alarm arose from above. It checked the pack from aiding the two attackers, but those two were too furious to be stopped. The skycraft cone shot down out of the sky; but it was too late. The fair-haired girl had

already killed one of her assailants and mortally
wounded the other. She did not wait to be
punished. Racing like the wind, she entered the
trees not thirty yards from where Thelon
crouched.

The portal at the base of the cone slid open and
one of the Hunters emerged. The throbbing alarm
changed pitch, and what was left of the hunting
pack darted away in pursuit. But instead of
pursuing the girl directly, they raced to surround
the grove. Then the gorilla-men dropped their
equipment and began shambling in a body toward
the grove.

Thelon glanced toward the Hunter. It had now
turned toward the portal; but its movements were
so jerky and spasmodic that he wondered if it was
really just some kind of machine. Then the
throbbing wail changed pitch again, and the
gorilla-men also spread out to surround the grove.
The girl would be trapped if she could not break
out of the grove, where her great speed would do
her no good. But he did not want to be trapped
himself, and slipped silently through the trees in
the direction of his canoe.

Then he saw the girl. She was standing with her
back to him, dagger in hand. She knew that she
was trapped; but like a lioness at bay was
determined to kill as many of her enemies as
possible before she herself was killed.

Only the gorilla-men entered the trees, issuing
guttural cries and beating the underbrush as they
advanced. The hunting pack circled outside, ready
to run the girl down should she break cover. The
ring was tightening; but Thelon was not yet

worried about his own escape. The gorilla-men were too slow and clumsy to catch him; the members of the hunting pack too fragile to fight him; to the Hunters he was just vermin, not worth their while. In any case, it was not him that they were after.

But could he rescue the girl? She would probably think that he was just another of her enemies and flee at the sight of him. He saw her turn and begin making her way toward the swamp, as if struck by some new idea. But she would not get far in those reptile-infested waters, even if she could swim. His suit of motley green rendered him almost invisible. He followed her silently through the trees.

There was a guttural cry just ahead, and a gorilla-man shambled out of the underbrush and tried to grab the girl. She dodged him easily; but his cry brought others closing in from all sides. The girl vanished into the shadows.

But a moment later she reappeared, plunging wildly through the trees with two gorilla-men shambling after her. She was coming right for him. He drew his bow and waited. Just as she reached him, he stepped from cover and dropped her nearest pursuer with an arrow through the forehead. The second caught an arrow through the right eye. Then he turned to catch up with the girl.

But she had stopped only a few yards away, and stood watching him like a wary jungle cat. The surest way to scare off a cat is to approach it directly. He beckoned to the girl, and turned in the direction of his canoe. There was not a sound behind him as he crept through the trees; although he was sure that the girl was following him. The gorilla-men were all around them now.

One of them shambled into view; there was no time to dodge into the shadows. The gorilla-man started to cry out just as Thelon fired. It was a hurried shot, and only caught him in the side of the neck. His strangled cries attracted the others, and soon the ring was too tight to break through. Thelon glanced over his shoulder. The girl stood only a few yards away, watching him.

He quickly led her out of sight, and pointed up into the foliage of an ancient oak tree. He sprang into the boughs and started to climb. He could hear the gorilla-men shambling through the underbrush nearby. But this time the girl did not follow him. She stood at the base of the tree, staring up at him. Evidently she did not know how to climb. He reached down and pulled her out of sight just as three gorilla-men came shambling out of the underbrush. They passed directly under the tree.

The girl seemed more comfortable when they had returned to the ground. She did not really trust him yet, but was intelligent enough to realize that he was her best chance of escape. She still held her dagger in her hand.

They reached the shore unseen. The reeds hiding the canoe were shoulder high, and both the gorilla-men and the hunting pack were now moving in the opposite direction.

But then a wailing alarm arose from the direction of the skycraft cone. The guttural cries of the gorilla-men instantly converged toward the shore; there were answering shouts from the hunting pack. Thelon hurried forward, no longer worried about concealment. Somehow the Hunters had detected them. He glanced at the metal collar around the girl's neck.

Dragging the canoe through the reeds and launching it was a matter of seconds. But they were now in open water. He started back upstream, trying to keep a grove of swamp oaks between himself and the skycraft cone.

He was still in the shallows when he heard someone splashing through the water after them. It was one of the hunting pack, the young man who had been one of the girl's original tormentors. He grabbed the stern of the canoe and tried to hold them back. In the flash of an eye the girl shot through the air and buried her dagger in his throat. Strangling and coughing blood, he vanished beneath the water.

Paddling for their lives, Thelon pulled the canoe out of the shallows. But the instant he reached deep water the wailing alarm from the skycraft cone changed pitch. The throng of gorilla-men milling about the shore turned and hurried in the opposite direction, back toward the cone. Had they given up? Or was the nature of the hunt going to be changed?

Though they were screened from both the cone section and the mother ship, Thelon sensed that their every move was somehow being monitored. He glanced again at the shimmering metal collar around the girl's neck.

She lounged at the stern of the canoe, carefully cleansing the blood from her dagger; her face was devoid of all expression. Only now did Thelon realize how really beautiful she was. Her fair hair was short and clean; it looked as if it had never known any comb but her fingers. She was no more than about nineteen years old, and stood only a few inches shorter than he did; her legs were unusually long and shapely. Her gray-green tunic was cut off at the shoulders and thighs, and on her small, high-arched feet she wore low shoes with sharp metal cleats on the bottom. Her eyes were jade green and disconcertingly feline. But that may have been an effect of their extreme alertness, combined with her face's total lack of expression. She said not a word.

There was still no sign of pursuit. Through a break in the trees he caught a quick glimpse of the skycraft cone. The three Hunters again stood in a line; the huge machines were again at their sides. He leaned into his paddle, expecting any moment to be entangled in a rain of stinging filaments. The canopy of the swamp forest would shelter them. It lay just ahead.

Then he heard the whine of engines about half a mile behind him. Six motor-launches were bearing down upon them; each precisely staffed with gorilla-men and members of the hunting pack. But the launches seemed to be steering themselves. There was nobody at the controls!

Thelon paddled the canoe out of sight, then doubled back through a maze of dark channels, using every advantage of natural cover to lose his pursuers. But he could not escape them. Whoever, or whatever, was steering the launches knew exactly where he was at all times. He entered a channel too narrow for the motorized craft to follow.

But it was a dead end, and he found himself

blocked by a narrow island that seemed to stretch for miles. Undulating rafts of some purplish water blossom covered the surface; it took all his strength to pull the canoe forward. The vegetation would not slow down the motor launches; they had found a wider inlet, and it was now too late to turn back. Fighting against the clinging vegetation with every stroke, he pulled for the narrow island.

Driving straight onto shore, he leaped out and pulled the girl after him. She still had her dagger in her hand; but though she stiffened at being touched, she did not use it. He let go of her arm and quickly dragged the light canoe across the narrow spit of land.

They reached the water again just as two women from the hunting pack came sprinting across the island toward them. The girl turned to fight, but Thelon shoved her into the canoe again and pushed off.

The two women halted at the water's edge. They were joined a moment later by the whole mob; but by then he had pulled the canoe safely out of reach. Neither the gorilla-men nor the hunting pack seemed to know what to do next. They milled up and back along the shore, restless and irresolute.

Then the wailing alarm arose once more, and the gorilla-men turned and shambled back toward the motor-launches; the hunting pack remained on shore. The launches were large and heavy, but Thelon knew that it would not take the powerful gorilla-men long to carry them across the island. And there could be no real hope of escape as long as the Hunters always knew where they were.

But how were they being monitored? He knew that the skycraft could see through total darkness. But through a dense forest? No, it had to be the girl's collar. Somehow it had to be removed. The only alternative was to beach the canoe and make a stand. But there were more gorilla-men than he had arrows in his quiver, and the final outcome was not in doubt. But how could the collar be removed?

Pulling the canoe against a hummock, he turned toward the girl. Her dagger was out in a flash. Despite everything that had happened, she would certainly try to kill him if he moved one step closer. Only later did he learn that this was merely a reflex, conditioned into her since childhood. There was no random breeding in the hunting pack.

The gorilla-men would take no more than fifteen or twenty minutes to port the motor-launches across the island. He tried talking to her; but she only stared expressionlessly at him. All he could think of at last was to pantomime removing a collar from his own neck and throwing it into the water.

She caught on at once; but her reaction surprised him. She took hold of the collar and pretended to pull it open, looking like somebody in terrible pain. Then she just stared at him, her face once more devoid of all expression.

He clearly did not know know what she meant; so she beckoned him closer and placed his hands on the collar. He tried to pull it open. The next thing he knew he was flat on his back at the bottom of the canoe, his arms numb to the elbow.

The shock had been no worse than that from the sting-fence, but he had not been prepared for it. The girl's jade-green eyes watched him with feline amusement.

He approached her again. She made no move to stop him, as if she thought he was just too stupid to have learned his lesson from the first shock. But the lesson he had learned was that he had pulled too hard. As with the sting-fence, action and reaction were proportional.

The collar was about an inch wide and perhaps half an inch thick; the shimmering gray-green metal was warm and slippery to touch. It was fastened with a simple hook-clasp at the back; but he broke out into a cold sweat as he reached for it. It was like facing the sting-fence all over again.

The whole world exploded into pain, maddening, stinging, will-sapping pain; blue lights flashed wildly across his brain. Then he was sitting in the bottom of the boat holding the collar in his hand. The pain had stopped the instant he rehooked the clasp; but for several moments he lay stunned and shaken.

It was an effort even to push the canoe from the hummock; his eyes only now began to focus again. He paddled until he found a deep lagoon, and dropped the collar overboard. The girl's face was still expressionless, but the look in her eyes was strangely intent. He smiled at her, but she just continued to stare at him.

Paddling through the galleries of dark swamp trees, he found a hummock from behind which they could see without being seen. There was no point in running now. If he had been wrong about the collar, this was as good a place as any to make a last stand. But the girl merely saw it as a fine opportunity for washing her legs and feet, dusty from the chase. All six motor-launches stopped in the lagoon, directly over the spot where he had dropped the collar.

Those on board looked at each other in confusion. Even the wailing alarm from the skycraft cone seemed indecisive. At last some of the gorilla-men stripped off their tunics and dived into the water. Two minutes passed before they surfaced; choking, coughing, but still emptyhanded. Then they dived again.

Thelon had no idea how long the Hunters would keep them diving; but their chances of ever finding the collar in the black ooze at the bottom of the lagoon did not seem very good. There was a sardonic glitter in the girl's eyes as she watched the uncouth figures dive again and again without success. Using the hummock as a screen, he turned and paddled silently away.

They came upon the ruins of an ancient town at dusk. A few of the buildings were still above water; the best preserved of all had once been a mansion. It would protect them from marauding reptiles for the night, and there was even a fire-place that still worked. He broiled some fish he had caught en route.

Meanwhile the girl strolled down to the water for a leisurely bath. Then she began prowling all over the old mansion, poking into every nook and cranny with the curiosity of a cat. She had a remarkable capacity for making herself comfort-able, and soon made a nest of old quilts and

blankets for herself on the only sound couch in the
only sound room in the mansion. What Thelon was
going to do for the night was apparently his business.

They ate by the light of the glowing coals of the
fireplace. The cries and screams of the swampland
reverberated through the darkness outside. He
tried talking to the girl again, but again she merely
stared at him. Perhaps she spoke a different
language.

He pointed to the coals and said, "Fire." No
reaction. Then he pointed to himself and said,
"Thelon." Still nothing. He tried several other
objects. All with the same result. The girl was
obviously intelligent. Was she just being coy?

At last she attempted to pronounce his name.
The closest she could come was something like
"Tullen." But at least it was a start. Slowly,
patiently, with much coaxing, he got her to repeat
several other words. She spoke like someone
unused to talking, pronouncing each word after
him with a heavy, lisping tongue. But when he
pointed at her, she again merely stared.

He sighed and slowly shook his head. Not only
had this beautiful, intelligent girl never learned to
talk, but apparently she did not even have a name.

"Well," he said, "then I'll just have to pick a
name for you." He thought of Walter Carswell's
wife, and named her Brenda.

"Brenda," she pronounced slowly, pointing to
herself.

CHAPTER XI: THE ARMY PEOPLE

It was a garden land; clear streams and lakes, green forests and meadows, abundant game. Corporal Sutton's map tracing started here, at the western edge of the Ozark Plateau. There had been no trace of wildmen for the last several days now. But the number and movements of the skycraft indicated that the Hunters had some kind of central base nearby, probably out on the Great Plains to the west.

The Army people had not survived for centuries by being easy to find. A stranger entering the Anomaly would have little chance of finding the stockade; he would probably find nothing but death. The Army people were sure to be at least as alert, and they had guns.

It was the middle of summer. The afternoon sun poured its golden warmth over the earth; but here in the shadows of the broadleaf forest it was still pleasantly cool. A small waterfall tumbled into the pond where Brenda sat naked on a rock, washing herself in the crystalline waters.

The girl had become a kind of pampered pet that tolerated him in exchange for food and protection. Clean and watchful and self-sufficient, with a remarkable knack for making herself comfortable in any situation, Thelon still could not approach her without triggering the reflex action of the drawn dagger — unless he warned her in advance. She had no idea where he was taking her, nor did she seem to care.

Through the long weeks of travel — out of the northern swampland, down the muddy, swollen waters of the Mississippi, and finally overland through the rolling hills and valleys of the Ozarks — the girl had not asked a single question. She could talk a little now, in a lisping, childlike way; but seldom spoke unless she wanted something.

The skycraft, increasing in numbers as they moved southwards, had ignored them. The wildmen, on the other hand, decreased in numbers to the south. Only once had they presented a real threat . . . .

Thelon had taken the girl hunting one morning. They had no luck at first, and came further inland from the river than he had intended. All at once a hairy, screaming, ragged band of wildmen appeared from behind a nearby hill. And the chase was on. The wildmen tried to cut them off from the river. Thelon was confident of his own speed and endurance; not since boyhood had anyone even come close to outrunning him. He knew that the girl was swift and agile; but they were miles from the river. Could she last?

She ran beside him with long, loping strides, and they soon outdistanced the wildmen. About a quarter mile from shore, she pulled ahead. Glancing back, she seemed to challenge him to keep up. He put on a burst of speed, but the instant he reached her she shot away like a young cougar, reaching the canoe well ahead of him. And she had not even been running hard!

When he finally came puffing up to the river, he found her seated in the front of the canoe, not in the stern where she normally sat. Only as he paddled from shore did he understand: in the front of the canoe she sat facing him. Her jade-green eyes sparkled with feline amusement. He could not tell which she enjoyed more, his humiliation in the race or his embarrassment at being stared at . . . .

Brenda slept the greater part of each day, sometimes as much as sixteen hours. Her waking hours were spent mainly in washing, making herself comfortable, and, lately, in preening. While exploring the ruins of a river city in what had once been Illinois, he had found a small hand-mirror. Thinking nothing of it, he gave it to the girl and continued to explore. But when he came back he found her still staring at her own reflection. Apparently she had never seen herself before.

She still had the mirror, her only possession aside from her clothes and her dagger; it now lay beside her on the rock where she was sitting. From time to time she would pick it up, holding it this way and that to look at herself from various

angles. At last she donned her tunic and sauntered
up the hill toward him. It was feeding time.

Game and fish were plentiful, wild berries and
nuts were in full season; they enjoyed a bountiful
meal together in the open. Then the girl curled up
and went to sleep. Though it was only late afternoon, he knew that she would sleep until the
following morning if left undisturbed.

Following the habits of a lifetime, he policed the
area, removing the faintest trace of their presence.
Brenda had left some footprints beside the pond;
these he carefully erased. It would take very sharp
eyes indeed to know that they had been here.

He sat down beneath a tree and unfolded his
map. The landscape was a vast expanse of forest
and meadow, unbroken as far as the eye could see,
even through binoculars. Did Corporal Sutton's
map tracing merely end at some familiar
landmark? Perhaps they were still many miles
short of the habitation of the Army people. He
wondered if they lived in some kind of stockade,
like the one in the Anomaly.

Deep in concentration on the map, he had not
heard a sound. Only when Brenda stirred did he
look up. They were surrounded! The girl leapt to
her feet, dagger drawn; her eyes flashed back and
forth, searching for an opening. But a solid
phalanx of grim-faced men dressed in khaki uniforms surrounded them, and they all had guns.

Strangers so discovered in the Anomaly would
have been summarily dealt with, and the soldiers
surrounding them had the ominous look of a firing
squad. Thelon knew that he had to act fast. All but
one of the soldiers wore striped insignia patches

like Corporal Sutton's. The single exception was a sallow, gray-haired little man, who wore a device consisting of two parallel gold bars on his collar.

"Captain," Thelon addressed him, "I come from the mine people who live far to the north beneath the ancient city of Compton. You sent an expedition to make contact with them some months ago." He noticed that the Captain seemed to understand what he was saying; he also noticed that the soldiers were glaring angrily at Brenda. "I'm afraid that the only one to reach Compton was a Corporal Sutton, who died soon afterwards. Here are his effects."

The Captain merely nodded, and a young man with a one-stripe patch on his arm took possession of the effects.

"How did they die?" demanded the Captain, and he too glanced angrily at Brenda. His dialect was clipped and nasal, but comprehensible.

Thelon explained quickly about Graydevil, how the monster had terrorized the Compton region, how it had finally been killed. All the while he was afraid that one of the soldiers would come too close to Brenda, who stood, dagger in hand, only a few yards away.

"Seven casualties, and nothing to show for it!" The Captain shook his head. "His Excellency won't like this. Not that we ever had any great hopes. The first expedition found the Compton district to be of low recruitment potential, though fairly populous. However, you look capable enough, young man. I see no reason why you shouldn't make a good soldier."

Then Thelon had an inspiration. He explained

where he actually came from, stressing his rank as
Mentor.

"Well, damn it, man," growled the Captain. "If
you'd give your report properly we wouldn't have
these problems."

But, as Thelon had hoped, his mention of having
held high rank seemed to have earned them a
reprieve. He had gone forth from the Anomaly in
search of knowledge; he had learned much during
his travels, and now had even discovered a
possible nucleus of resistance against the
Hunters. Despite their incredible power, earth
was a hostile environment; perhaps they were
vulnerable in some unknown way. He did not want
any mistakes now.

"Friends, Brenda," he pronounced slowly and
clearly. "Friends."

The girl had always done pretty much as she
pleased; but this time she surprised him.
Sheathing her dagger, she moved docilely to his
side. It was the first gesture of real trust that she
had shown him.

The Captain barked an order, the ranks of
soldiers closed around them, and they were
marched down the slopes. But no sooner had they
reached the base of the hill than the Captain called
a halt. The turf at their feet lifted like an awning,
revealing a long tunnel. So that was how they had
been taken unawares! The whole troop marched
silently inside, and the turf awning was again
lowered into place.

The tunnel was of white-washed brick, lined
with lanterns; the concrete floors were scrubbed
and spotless. As they turned the corner they came

upon a work detail of men and women in blue denim uniforms. They had been scrubbing the walls and floor; but the instant the soldiers appeared they leaped to their feet and began bowing and scraping, servile grins on their emaciated faces. The soldiers ignored them.

The Captain called a halt in front of a row of metal doors. "Disarm the cat and throw her in here!" he ordered, and a sergeant stepped forward.

"No, Brenda!" Thelon cried.

But it was too late; her reflexes were just too quick. Fortunately, the sergeant ducked just fast enough to catch the dagger thrust on the side of the neck, rather than straight into his throat. Brenda was instantly overwhelmed, disarmed, and locked into the cell. The sergeant was bleeding, but the wound did not look too serious.

Thelon was also disarmed; but the Captain evidently had other plans for him. Dismissing the platoon, he kept two soldiers as guards and led the way into an adjacent tunnel.

This soon opened onto a ramp circling an enormous underground silo, several storeys deep. Then Thelon recalled reading of the missile weapons of the time of Walter Carswell, how these had been fired ineffectually at the skytankers that had poisoned the earth. Perhaps some of those missiles had been fired from this very silo. But there were no missiles here now.

The Captain halted in front of a metal door, which read in neat white letters, "Col. Lyndon R. Bradford, U.S.A." He rapped smartly and opened it.

At a desk facing the door sat a pale young man with a two-stripe insignia patch on his arm. He jumped to his feet and saluted.

"The Colonel's expecting you now, sir," he said in a clipped, nasal voice. Then he scooted to a door at the left side of the office, servilely holding it open while the Captain passed inside.

The two guards never took their eyes off Thelon. They were both privates, although one had gray hair. There was an almost sterile order and cleanliness about the office, and a work detail was even now scrubbing the floor. None of them dared to raise his eyes. Several minutes passed before the office door reopened.

The Captain beckoned from the doorway. "All right, the Colonel will see you now. Step lively."

Thelon was roughly shoved forward by the guards. Behind a polished desk sat a florid, balding little man with a white mustache. He eyed Thelon contemptuously.

"He's big enough, Kennelly," he said. "Don't get recruits this size much any more. He'll take some cleaning up, though. We don't allow hair or beards like that in this man's army. You say he had a cat with him when you picked him up?"

"Yes, sir," replied the Captain. "Stabbed a sergeant while he was in process of carrying out his orders."

The Colonel shook his head. "The wonder is how they got past so many units without being spotted. I don't like this at all, Kennelly."

"No, sir."

"Penetrated to Center. Right through our whole ring of sites. If I know His Excellency, Kennelly, there'll be some personnel going to the wall for this. We're in the clear, though. Good work, Captain!''

"Thank you, sir." The Captain looked quite pleased with himself.

"Don't know why you brought in the cat, though. You know our standing orders.''

The Captain glanced shiftily at Thelon, and whispered something in the Colonel's ear. Thelon tensed: the words "standing orders" had an ominous ring.

"Ah, so that's it," said the Colonel, nodding his bald head. "Then you were quite right, Kennelly. This could be a feather in the cap of the whole unit. Never had one that could talk before. And you actually heard her talk, eh?''

Again the Captain whispered in his ear. Thelon could no longer keep silent.

"Colonel," he said, "the girl knows only a few words, nothing more. I came here —''

"Silence!" screamed the Captain.

"Turn the cat over to the Chaplain's boys," ordered the Colonel, as if Thelon were beneath his notice. "They're good at getting confessions. And the timing couldn't have been better. If we can bring any new information to the General Court Martial tomorrow, there should be awards and promotions in it for all of us. Yes, Kennelly, you were quite right in bringing the cat back with you. And the Chaplain's boys needn't be too gentle about it," he added significantly.

"No, sir: They'll get whatever she knows about the Shakies out of her.''

"You mean you're going to torture the girl?''

Thelon exploded. "This is not only inhuman, it's stupid. How can this poor girl confess when she can barely talk? I've asked her about the Hunters, or *Shakies* as you apparently call them, and she knows nothing but —"

"Silence!" screamed the Captain again, this time drawing his pistol.

But Thelon was too angry now. "I've been silent long enough. I don't know what's going on here, but I'm not a recruit and I don't intend —"

The rifle-butt caught him just behind the right ear. There was a stunning flash of light, the whole room spun giddily about, and the floor seemed to leap up at him. Then darkness . . . .

The next thing he knew he was lying on a bare canvas cot in the corner of some kind of dormitory. The back of his head ached; his eyes did not seem to want to focus. Slowly, painfully, he sat up, holding his head in his hands.

"Well, well," growled somebody nearby. "Looks like Sleeping Beauty's finished his nap." Several others laughed at this.

Thelon now realized that there were a number of other people in the dormitory. They were of various ages; but all wore the same type of uniform. A bulldog-faced sergeant hovered over him.

"Let's go, Sleeping Beauty," he growled. "You've got a date with the barber. I don't know where they get you jewels." He shook his bulldog jowls. "You recruits get worse every year. Now move!"

Thelon rose groggily to his feet. There was a tender spot behind his right ear, but little swelling. Somebody kicked a chair toward him, and he was thrust down from behind; a towel was wrapped around his neck, and a wiry little man went to work with clippers and razor. Then, in rapid succession, he was stripped and shoved into the shower room, fitted with a uniform, given dog-tags stamped with the name "Arthur S. Weil," and assigned a bunk and locker. By the time they had finished with him, he was the very model of an army private. It was just time for taps.

Armed guards were posted inside the dormitory; the door was locked from the outside. The only light came from the lantern over the latrine door. Thelon thought mostly about Brenda before he fell asleep; but there was nothing he could do now to help her. There seemed no chance of escape.

It was in the chow hall the next morning that he received orders to attend the General Court Martial; he was to wear his full-dress uniform. Most of the soldiers regarded him with contempt, the contempt of the veteran for the recruit; but a few of the younger privates talked to him.

As far as he could gather, the officer class was hereditary; a system of impressment filled the ranks with recruits such as himself; all servile labor was performed by work details, who were slaves in all but name. The "Shakies" were indeed nearby; but there seemed to be no thought of ever really fighting them. It was just militarism for the sake of militarism: hereditary, self-seeking, self-perpetuating militarism as an end in itself. This was not the nucleus of resistance he had hoped for.

The General Court Martial was held in a large

white-washed hall. He entered, flanked by two armed guards. More armed guards flanked a crowd of forty or so men and women, dressed in blue denim and huddled forlornly in front of a polished oak tribunal which stretched from one side of the hall to the other. The tribunal was still empty. But it reminded him of accounts he had read of the ancient English Sessions, where scores of men, women, and even children were summarily sentenced to death.

Then he saw Brenda. She was dressed in a uniform of blue denim; her right eye was black and swollen, her lower lip was cut. But she looked more defiant than ever, a proud jade-eyed goddess among a huddle of forlorn wretches.

She recognized him even in his uniform and without his long hair and beard. She looked expressionlessly at him for a moment, as if to see that he was all right; then turned away.

Then the Captain stepped forward at the right side of the tribunal and barked, "Attention!" Heels clicked and rifles snapped all about the crowded hall as two doors, one on each side of the tribunal, simultaneously swung open.

"His Excellency General Douglas R. Gratham IV," announced the Captain, and recited a string of titles — defender of this and commander of that. Then: "His Eminence Chaplain Preston Staley Warrington III," and he recited another string of titles — protector of this and counselor of that.

Then two middle-aged men strutted simultaneously into the hall from opposite sides of the tribunal. The General was gaudy with ribbons,

medals, and festoons of gold braid; the Chaplain,
although wearing a humble army uniform, was
radiant with medallions of various kinds. Both
looked sleek and bumptious. They seated themselves simultaneously at the center of the tribunal,
while their respective underlings filed in from
each side.

Thelon watched the "Chaplain's boys," who
were supposed to have gotten a "confession" from
Brenda. Then he noticed that Brenda was edging
stealthily to the outside of the crowd facing them.
They had taken her dagger from her, but he sensed
that she had a weapon of some kind. Like a
wounded lioness, she was silently stalking her
enemies. She would not die alone.

The General rapped with a gavel, although the
hall was already deathly silent. "With the accord
of Chaplain Warrington" — the Chaplain nodded
solemnly — "I declare this General Court Martial
now in session. Offenses against the Uniform Code
of Military Justice will now be read."

A tall, scrawny man with ferrety eyes rose from
the Chaplain's side of the tribunal and circled to
the front. Accepting a sheet of paper from the
Chaplain, he turned and read the names and
offenses of each of the huddled, whimpering
crowd before him. The most common offenses
were malingering, insubordination, and overage.
Then he read, "No name, collaboration," which
Thelon assumed referred to Brenda.

There was no evidence presented, no witnesses
or cross-examination, no defense of any kind. The
charges read, the General and Chaplain went
through a show of conferring together. After

several minutes of solemn nodding and whispering, they both sat back simultaneously. Again the General rapped his gavel to the deathly-silent hall.

"With the accord of Chaplain Warrington" — again the Chaplain nodded solemnly — "sentence will now be passed."

This time it was the Captain who approached the tribunal. He accepted a pre-written sheet of paper from the General. But before reading it he whispered something to the General, who immediately relayed the message to the Chaplain. All three officers looked at Thelon for a moment.

Then the Captain turned toward the huddled crowd and announced: "The sentence of this General Court Martial is death by firing squad. Sentence to be carried out immediately." A pathetic wail arose from the crowd. Ignoring them, the Captain began a second announcement: "The new recruit will now be brought forward for the purpose . . ." But he never finished.

Brenda seemed almost to fly out of the crowd. Something flashed in her hand, and the scrawny, ferrety-eyed man fell coughing and choking to the floor, his throat slashed from ear to ear. Smashing his fists left and right, Thelon knocked down his two guards. Using one of their rifles as a club, he bludgeoned the guards in front of him.

There was shouting and confusion. The monolithic discipline of only a moment ago collapsed into chaos. People swarmed this way and that as in a hive of angry bees. Brenda was jabbing and slashing wildly at the "Chaplain's boys." The Captain drew his pistol, but Thelon

clubbed him to the ground before he could fire,
snatching the pistol in mid-air. Two quick strides
and he vaulted the tribunal. Grabbing the
confused General by the scruff of the neck, he
jammed the pistol against his forehead.

"Attention!" he cried.

The inbred discipline of generations brought the
turmoil to a sudden halt. There was even some
clicking of heels. But this did not halt Brenda. She
bounded across the tribunal like a lynx, straight
for the Chaplain's throat, knife flashing.

"No, Brenda!" Thelon shouted.

But instead of cutting the Chaplain's throat, she
grabbed him by the hair and merely held her knife
against his windpipe. Then she looked to Thelon
for their next move. The knife was only a common
table knife, but it had been honed to a razor edge;
probably against the walls of her cell. Neither the
General nor the Chaplain showed any sign of fight.

But there was still some spirit in the ranks.
Once more the turmoil erupted all over the hall;
but this time it was some of the soldiers
themselves who were wresting the weapons from
the guards and thrusting them against the wall.
Nearly a third of the soldiers rebelled. They too
now looked to him for their next move.

"Order your men into the chamber to the right,"
he told the General, who complied instantly.

"Do what he says!" the Chaplain screeched,
prompted by the pressure of a sharpened table-
knife against his windpipe. Brenda was
remarkably alert.

So were some of the others. As the disarmed
soldiers and what was left of the "Chaplain's

boys" filed from the hall, a ring of keys was produced, the chamber into which they were filing emptied of weapons, and all exits locked. Only two of the rebel soldiers held a rank as high as corporal. Thelon beckoned to one of them.

"Do you know the way to the surface?"

"Yes, sir. But it's sure to be blocked by now."

"Do you think they'll fire on the General and Chaplain?"

"No, sir."

"Then lead the way. We'll be right behind you with the hostages in plain sight. You," he called to the other corporal, "take two of your men and bring up the rear. Let's go!"

"Yes, yes! All right! I'm coming!" moaned the Chaplain as Brenda bounced him around to the front of the tribunal. There was no doubt in his mind that "No name, collaboration" meant business.

They had hardly left the hall when they were confronted by an armed company. Then they heard the tramp of more soldiers double-timing up from the rear. Thelon did not hesitate. His orders were relayed by the terrified, quavering voice of the General:

"Stand aside with your men, lieutenant! Please don't argue, or they'll shoot me."

"Yes, yes!" cried the Chaplain. "Stand aside!"

The armed company obeyed, retreating into an adjacent passageway with clockwork precision. But as Thelon's troop trotted by, several of the rankers ran forward and joined them. Their lieutenant made no move to stop them.

They reached the surface without further opposition. It was an overcast day, threatening rain. But Thelon did not like the idea of concentrating so many people together in the open. Important hostages would be nothing to the Hunters; although sixty or seventy refugees might. He called a halt beside a stream about a mile from the ancient missile site.

"All right, General," he said. "Let's have one thing clear. Your only chance of living lies in our safe escape. Make no mistake about that. Once out of your territory, you have my word that you will be freed unharmed. Now, which is the safest route back to the river?"

The General was ready to tell everything he knew; the Chaplain was positively anxious. From the way Brenda hovered around him with her knife, he may even have played a personal part in giving her the black eye and cut lip. But neither man seemed to know very much; it was doubtful if either had been above ground in the last thirty years. The Chaplain glanced nervously at Brenda; the General looked ready to cry from sheer annoyance.

"Perhaps I can help," said a pale, gaunt man dressed in the blue-denim uniform of the condemned. "My name is Drucker, Robert E. Drucker. Nine years ago I came to this region to establish contact with these people, just as you did. I'm from the Cave Cities, in what was once Kentucky."

Thelon nodded. "What information do you have? For instance, do you know of a safe route back to the river?"

"Not by the way you came, Thelon," he whispered. "We know all about you through the grapevine. But if you're really going to let these two go, we'd better talk in private. There'll be enough reprisals for this escape as there is."

There was a soft patter of raindrops in the trees overhead. Drucker led the way out of earshot.

"Our only chance is to circle to the west," he said. "You must be some woodsman to have gotten through the defenses of eight sites; but now they'll be looking for you." He added wryly, "I didn't get two miles from the river before they captured me."

"But isn't it mostly open plains to the west?"

"Yes, but all the missile sites there were swept clean by the Aliens generations ago. Center is the westernmost occupied site. I've peeked at their maps, Thelon. You yourself might slip through their defenses, and maybe the girl. But not this many people."

"But won't our hostages get us through?"

"From what I hear, there are a couple of colonels who would just love to see this pair shot. It would all be accidental, of course. Probably during some kind of phony rescue attempt. No, our only chance is circling to the west."

Thelon's own map (now unfortunately lost) and certain clues he had picked up while being "re-cruited" tended to confirm what the man said.

"All right," he decided at last. "West it is. You said something about the Cave Cities. Can you find your way back? And would we be welcome there?"

"Yes to both questions. But first we have to get back to the river. From there I know the way." Then he knelt down and drew a crude map in the damp sand beside the stream.

The Cave Cities, it turned out, were less than

two hundred miles east of the river. Food would be no problem at this time of year. Their numbers would intimidate the wildmen; but such numbers would also put them in constant danger of being netted by the Hunters.

The skills of concealment he had learned in the Anomaly might protect them. But it would take time to organize supply and defense systems, to train scouts and make the hooded cloaks of bark and grass that would allow them to blend into the landscape. Their immediate need was some shelter that would both screen them from skycraft and be beyond the reach of any "rescue" attempt by ambitious colonels. A ruined city near the edge of the plains was the obvious answer.

But Drucker informed him that every town for hundreds of miles around had long since been cannibalized to provide supplies and building materials for the missile site complex. There was not a wall or roof left standing above ground anywhere in the forest.

"What about one of the old missile sites?" he suggested. "They've been empty for generations, and our brave boys in khaki never venture out onto the plains. Standing orders. I don't know what's left of them, but there's one only a few miles from here. It's out on the plains, but it's an overcast day and we should be safe from the spaceships of the Aliens."

Thelon knew better; but this was no time to argue the point. Even if they had to risk crossing a few miles of open plain, as abandoned missile site sounded like their best chance. They certainly could not stay here much longer.

"Let's get moving!" he cried.

CHAPTER XII:
THE MACHINES THAT WAITED

Thelon watched the scouts returning from the ancient missile site. Two broad bands of willow trees bordered a small stream to the north; they provided cover to within a few hundred yards of the site. Not much was left above ground; there were no roofs and few walls still standing. Any shelter they might find lay below ground.

He lowered his binoculars. The missile site was less than two miles out on the open plain; but because of their detour to the north, it would be some time yet before the scouts reported back. He had had the refugees gather nuts and berries as they trooped through the forest. At the base of the hill where he stood he could see them now collecting the grass and bark they would later use to sew into camouflage cloaks. The General and the Chaplain seemed to be doing most of the heavy

work. But everything still depended upon the
report of the scouts.

He glanced back at Brenda. She lay curled
asleep beneath a bush; it still amazed him how
much sleep she got each day. No less amazing was
the energy she possessed during her few waking
hours. But she had lost some of her feline com-
posure, and often seemed troubled by some inner
conflict whenever he approached her now. There
was still no conflict when any other man came too
close, however. The dagger was out in a flash.

The central base of the Hunters was close. How
close, not even Drucker knew. But he did know
that this was not their only base on the planet.
They had at least one more, in Africa. There were
also civilized people still alive somewhere on that
continent. About every ten years, Drucker
informed him, the people of the Cave Cities would
exchange radio messages with a station there at a
prearranged time and date. It only took the
skycraft a few minutes to home in on the signal; so
the transmitter had to be set up hundreds of miles
away, and the messages were all too brief. But at
least there were civilized people still alive in
Africa. The other continents were silent.

Thelon recalled the autumn round-ups of the
mammoth game animals in the Barren Lands and
the automated corral in the swamplands to the
north that would house the giant reptiles during
the cold season. The skycraft were almost never
seen during the winter months. Did the Hunters
simply pick up and move with the sun, leaving
their incredible machines to tend their no less
incredible game animals until the following

season? Was the earth no more to them than a
kind of hunting resort, with game animals from all
over the galaxy? And were human beings no more
to them than vermin to be gassed out of existence
or bred and trained as men once bred and trained
foxhounds and mules? It was hard to accept.

The scouts were nearly to the forest now; he had
sent two of the rebel soldiers. The poor wretches
in blue denim were already exhausted from their
hike through the forest. Years of overwork and
malnutrition had left them incapable of sustained
effort. They needed food and rest before they
started on the long trek to the Cave Cities.

The instant Thelon started down the hill,
Brenda was awake and on her feet. Together they
picked their way through the trees and underbrush. The sky was still overcast, but it had
stopped raining.

The report of the scouts was favorable; they had
even discovered some lanterns and a supply of
kerosene. But there was a lot of debris around the
entrance to the underground silo. Thelon sent
most of the rebel soldiers ahead to clear this; he
himself led the main body of refugees. Despite all
he could do to hurry them on, it took well over an
hour to reach the site. No skycraft appeared.

The rebel soldiers were clearing the last of the
debris away from the entrance as the weary band
straggled in off the plain. But there was no time to
rest. Thelon would not relax until he had the last
of them safely below ground. He had used all his
skills of woodcraft to cover their trail through the
forest; but they had only been able to gather food
for a couple of days. He would have to lead a
foraging party as soon as possible. Right now, he

wanted a good look around the silo before they settled down.

A concrete stairway, which had probably been only an emergency exit originally, wound downwards from the center of a shattered concrete bunker. Kerosene lanterns had been lit and spaced along the walls. The dust of generations covered everything like a gray carpet.

He joined some of the rebel soldiers in a cavernous hall; but the bulk of the refugees still huddled on the stairway, tired and frightened, unable to turn back and afraid to go forward. Brenda padded restlessly up and back; her jade-green eyes alert, missing nothing. Thelon turned to one of the corporals.

"See if you can't get the others down here," he said, his voice echoing strangely through the silence. "But take it easy, they're nearly exhausted. I'm going to have a look around."

Picking up one of the lanterns, he crossed the hall and entered a dark passageway. Brenda was right behind him. Most of the doors had been ripped from their hinges as if by some inescapable tentacle; heavy desks and cabinets had been tossed about; the chow hall was a riot of scattered trays, tables, and benches. Not one human being had been left behind.

But this had all happened long ago. It looked safe enough now, and Thelon leaned over the steel railing and peered down into the deep central well. It was empty; the missiles here too had probably all been fired in a vain attempt to bring down the skytankers. This site may have been uninhabited for centuries. He was just turning away when he heard the sound.

"Tullen!" cried Brenda.

But he needed no warning. He had heard the hum of drover machines before. He raced back toward the hall, with Brenda at his side.

"It's a trap!" he shouted. "Back to the surface!"

Screaming and jostling, the refugees fought their way back up the stairway they had just left. Thelon had no idea what they would find waiting for them at the top, but they could not stay here.

The whisper of metal wheels on dust-blanketed concrete was growing louder; the hum of machinery, waiting for just this moment, was now converging from all over the silo. The Hunters had left caretakers after their first netting here, caretakers that would wait indefinitely, until the presence of a critical number of humans triggered them into operation.

Did this critical number also trigger some alarm to the skycraft? He was too busy hurrying the people up the stairway to worry about it now. Some way he had to prevent the drover machines from following them to the surface. There was concrete rubble scattered all about the ruins above. Could they reblock the entrance in time? The exhausted refugees were maddeningly slow.

A giant face glided out of the darkness, coming right at them with its four mechanical arms outstretched. Brenda no longer wore the collar of the Hunters, and the drover machine turned in pursuit. She had seen such machines all her life; but they had never attacked her before. She dodged it at the last instant.

Before the machine could whirl around, Thelon snatched up a kerosene lantern and smashed it against the casing behind the huge painted face.

Then he too was dodging for his life. Brenda seemed more concerned with his safety than her own. Following his example, she also smashed a lantern against the rear of the machine. It was now a raging pillar of fire; but still it pursued them.

Then another giant face glided out of the darkness; then a third. Thelon could only run and dodge for his life; but the girl was swifter and much more agile. She had time to snatch up the remaining lanterns, circle the onrushing faces, and set them ablaze from behind. But now the drover machines were coming from all directions.

"Brenda!" he shouted. "Go!"

She dodged under the arms of an onrushing machine and followed him to the stairs. The blazing machine was right behind them, and the stairway ahead was still blocked! The refugees had not quite reached the surface! But just as they reached the highest landing there was a sharp *click* behind them. The machine stopped, blocking the stairway with its burning wreckage. The machines just behind it immediately began tearing it to pieces, trying to clear the way; although some of them were also afire. That gave them enough time to reach the surface.

"Get going!" he ordered, the instant the soldiers had finished blocking the entrance. "Carry the ones who can't keep up if you have to, but get going! I don't want anybody left behind!"

But he himself stayed behind, listening for any sound of digging from below, his eyes alert for any sign of skycraft from above. Brenda remained faithfully by his side. Minutes passed. Then all at once the earth began to tremble; the machines had at last cleared the wreckage, and mechanical arms were now attacking the rubble from below. But the stairway near the surface was too narrow for more than one machine to work at a time.

He glanced across the plain. The soldiers had caught up with the others, and the whole troop was now plodding as fast as they could back toward the forest. The willows straddling the small river screened them from above, and once into the trees they would be safe from the drover machines.

"Brenda!" he cried. "Let's go!"

And they raced like the wind across the plain. The girl had cut up her blue denim uniform until it was a ragged facsimile of the leather tunic she normally wore. He could never have kept up with her swift, loping strides if she had not chosen to hang back. They reached the willows in record time, and they were just fast enough.

The giant cone dropped out of the clouds like a bomb, decelerating with crushing speed directly over the missile site. Thelon could have reached the trees in minutes; the girl even sooner. But they brought up the rear of the troop, urging them on, seeing that the old and weary were not left behind. They were still a mile from the forest when the cone settled to earth.

A moment later the portal opened and out flew the hunting pack. Gangs of gorilla-men began hauling the huge machines into place. To the Hunters this was evidently just so much sport. Their hunting pack rushed across the plain with terrible swiftness.

"Fall back!" cried Thelon. "You men with rifles! Try and pick off the leaders!" He glanced at

Brenda, but her jade-green eyes only flashed with anger. She had no love for the hunting pack.

Either the marksmanship or the weapons of the soldiers were faulty, but it took several volleys to bring down even a few of the hunting pack. Three of them lay dead in a gulley nearby. More ominous was the fact that the gorilla-men had finished positioning the netting machines and were now working to clear the debris blocking the missile site entrance. The refugees were still several hundred yards from the trees, many stumbling from exhaustion. The willows straddling the river would not save them from being netted.

"Catch up with the others," Thelon ordered the soldiers. "Tell them to scatter." He took one of the rifles and a few spare clips. "Hurry!"

There was no way he could get Brenda to leave with them. A throbbing wail arose from the sky-craft cone as he led her back toward the missile site, using the river bank as a screen. He kept up a steady fire as long as his ammunition lasted. He was a far more formidable marksman with a bow, but still managed to pick off several of the gorilla-men. The hunting pack had taken cover out on the rolling plain. No Hunter appeared beside a netting machine.

But he knew that their weaponry must go far beyond mere netting machines; this was just a sport with them. Human hunters had also once endured discomforts and hostile environments for the sake of their sport. He glanced back. The refugees had now scattered, making the netting machines impracticable; many had reached the trees. He and Brenda would follow them in a minute or two. Then he noticed Brenda fumbling with a spare clip, trying to reload it. He slipped down the river bank to help her. It was at that moment that the force beam struck.

Trees, rocks, bushes, the whole top of the river bank, simply dissolved. He and Brenda were left stunned and glassy-eyed; a rain of dust and ashes fell about them. The Hunters indeed had other weapons than their nets. It was time to leave.

Again using the river bank as a screen, they dodged in and out of the willows as they raced for the forest. But he had to know what was happening. Peering cautiously between some boulders near the top of the bank, he saw that a Hunter now stood in the mouth of the cone's portal.

The throbbing wail had changed pitch, and the plains were a nightmare of speeding machines. The drover machines had been freed; the hunting pack raced behind them, using them as a shield. Two columns of gray-green vehicles packed with gorilla-men spread out like a great pincers; but one of the vehicles was speeding straight for the river bank. Nobody was driving it.

There was no longer any hope of reaching the forest; both he and Brenda were trapped. The rebel soldiers would give a good account of themselves in the dense forest; few if any of the refugees would be captured. He had stymied the Hunters just long enough; but he knew that he could not beat them. His only chance, and Brenda's, was to join them. The Army people may have saved his life by shaving off his hair and beard.

He fired a full clip into the speeding vehicle; then dived down the slope as the force beam destroyed the river bank above him. The vehicle had veered in his direction, despite the fact that he had killed or wounded all the gorilla-men inside. Then he led the way back toward the gulley where the three members of the hunting pack lay dead. Brenda followed without question; she too seemed to realize that they would never reach the forest alive.

Thelon was taller and more muscular than any member of the hunting pack; but without his long hair and beard he hoped to pass undetected. In fact, it was unlikely that the Hunters could detect any but glaring differences between one human being and another. The drover machines were another matter. They would detect any living presence not wearing a metal collar, and there was no hiding from them. He began tearing off pieces of his army uniform as he ran; again Brenda followed his lead. By the time they reached the gulley they were both stark naked.

The dead male was only an inch or two shorter than he was. But how were the tunic and cleated shoes fastened? It was now Brenda's turn to take the lead. Her quick intelligence had caught his intentions at once, and she began stripping two of the bodies. He had a lot to learn about the ways of the hunting pack; but soon they were both dressed in tunics of gray-green leather. No earth animal that he knew of produced leather so soft and fine.

He crept to the top of the gulley. The Hunter stood before the portal of the skycraft cone like some obscene idol. A gang of gorilla-men were combing the river bank; but the drover machines had stopped short of the trees. Bursts of rifle fire echoed out of the forest. Not a single refugee had been captured.

But as he looked about him, he could feel a growing hollowness in the pit of his stomach; beads of perspiration broke out on his forehead; his palms grew moist, and his hands trembled. There was no evading the ordeal that now faced him. He climbed slowly back down to the bottom of the gulley. Brenda watched him expressionlessly.

He took hold of the collar and slowly, ever so slowly, eased open its clasp. The whole world seemed to explode in pain and flashing blue lights; but he persisted. A moment later he was sitting with the collar in his hand, weak and shaken. With trembling fingers he fastened it about Brenda's neck. Then he knelt beside the body of the dead male.

But he could not bring himself to face the slamming concussion of pain again. Three times he took hold of the collar; three times he sat back, perspiring and trembling. Before he could stop her, Brenda darted forward and tried to yank the collar open. She was knocked sprawling, almost unconscious. Her jade-green eyes looked up at him, dazed and helpless.

A new throbbing wail arose from the skycraft cone, and Brenda signaled to him that the hunting pack was being recalled. But still he could not bring himself to face the ordeal. Evading it, he again crept to the top of the gulley to look around.

The hunting pack loped swiftly back across the plains, less than half a mile away. There were fewer gorilla-men in the vehicles now emerging from the forest. The soldiers had indeed given a good account of themselves. But now the drover machines turned back toward the missile site; a score of giant faces moving with blinding speed across the rolling plain. Then one of them turned in his direction. He had been detected.

He reached the naked body just as the giant face began to raise its claw-like hands for a grip from which there would be no escape. There was a gasp from Brenda, but it was lost in the explosion of pain and flashing lights. Then he was sitting with the collar clasped about his neck, stunned with the shock. But the drover machine lowered its metal arms and veered back into line with the others. He had been accepted as a member of the hunting pack.

"Tullen!" cried Brenda, springing away from him.

At the far end of the gulley, not fifty yards away, appeared the leaders of the hunting pack. They glanced curiously at the stripped bodies, but then loped swiftly away. Thelon ran after them. Brenda followed, careful not to stay too close to him. Once more he marveled at the girl's quick intelligence.

They reached the end of the gulley just in time to fall in at the rear of the pack. The drover machines were nowhere in sight, probably having returned to their long vigil underground. The gorilla-men were hauling the last of the gray-green vehicles through the open portal of the skycraft cone. But the Hunter was gone, and Thelon breathed a sigh of relief. Perhaps when he had fully recovered from the shock of removing the collars he would be ready to face one. But he was glad that it did not have to be right now.

He loped along at what he thought was a fair imitation of the running style of the hunting pack. But Brenda was not satisfied. She spent the last

few hundred yards to the skycraft cone giving him
an impromptu lesson in the art of running. It was
important that he at least ran like the rest of the
hunting pack; although he knew that he could
never match their speed.

They were the last to arrive. It was dim inside,
like the light under many feet of water. Rows of
narrow stalls ran all around the tapering interior;
ramps spiraled downward to the very base of the
metal deck, which would probably be opened
somehow when the cone rejoined the mother ship
somewhere above the clouds. He could just make
out the stalls opposite the portal. These were
reserved for the gorilla-men, who already stood in
their assigned places, stolid and obedient.

The hunting pack were more temperamental;
they jostled each other skittishly, reluctant to
enter their stalls. But at last they too began to file
into their assigned places. Thelon tried to slip un-
noticed into an empty stall, but a hiss from Brenda
saved him from what might have been a fatal
blunder. The females were kept in a different tier
of stalls from the less numerous males. He dived
into the empty stall Brenda indicated, wondering
what happened next.

But no sooner was he inside than hundreds of
filaments shot out of the bulkheads all around
him, gently encasing every part of his body in a
soft network. Without warning the deck dropped
away, and he found himself as helpless as a fly in a
spider-web.

Then he felt himself sinking slowly downwards
as the filaments encasing him absorbed the effects
of acceleration. He had left the earth.

CHAPTER XIII: THE HUNTING PACK

The other members of the hunting pack were mildly curious about Thelon at first; but lost interest once they could identify him. They slept the greater part of each day; their waking hours were largely taken up with eating, washing, and being groomed by the gorilla-men who serviced the kennels. Thelon was housed with nine other males. But none of them could talk, and he had no means of gathering information.

He did not even know where he was. The flight had been a short one; when the web of filaments encasing him had withdrawn into the bulkheads, he found himself — and the entire skycraft! —inside a structure so vast that he could not even guess its dimensions. There were no openings into the outside world. The walls and floor were all of the shimmering gray-green metal; all equipment was heavily shielded, grounding cables were attached everywhere. But most surprising of all, the Hunters were now able to move about easily; there was none of the spasmodic jerkiness that had made all their movements outside the structure so grotesque.

The front of his kennel was sealed with a sting-fence, as he painfully discovered the first time he approached it. A number of females were kept in a large kennel somewhere nearby; but he did not see Brenda again until the day of his first hunt — and almost his last.

The lighting in the kennels simulated night and day; thus three days passed before he heard the wailing alarm. At first he did not know what it meant; but when the others bounded to their feet, he had no choice but to follow them up the ramp and into his stall in the skycraft cone. The mother ship itself was evidently docked somewhere higher up in the structure. He was a member of the hunting pack now, and would be expected to act accordingly.

This was also the first hunt for the three males and eight females who had replaced those killed in the skirmish by the missile site. He was stronger and smarter than they were; although he lacked their incredible speed and agility. But they had been specially bred and trained, and he would have to keep his eyes open. Fortunately for him, Brenda was also keeping her eyes open.

By running as hard as he could, Thelon was able to keep up with the stalking speed of the pack. Their quarry was of the same species as Graydevil; he saw the monster loping through the brush like

a giant hyena. Unlike Graydevil, it did not have a
crippled paw.

The hunting pack at last brought it to bay on a
sandy rise scattered with shrubs. Thelon did his
best to imitate them, as they dodged and leaped
and circled about the monster. Some of them even
darted in to jab it with their daggers.

But he made the mistake of judging this
creature's speed by that of the crippled Graydevil.
The swipe of its great talons would surely have
torn him to pieces had not Brenda, at the risk of
her own life, darted straight past its jaws and
stabbed it in the leg. It was distracted just long
enough for him to dodge out of range.

Two females were brought down before the
monster was at last netted. As the throbbing wail
from the skycraft cone recalled the hunting pack,
Thelon knew all too well that there would have
been a third slashed and broken body left behind
had not Brenda risked her life to save him. He also
understood now why all the gorilla-men and
members of the hunting pack he had seen thus far
were so young. Human beings meant no more to
the Hunters than dogs or horses had once meant
to human beings. They were cheap and
expendable.

The Hunters seemed to be arriving and depart-
ing regularly from this their planetary hunting
resort; perhaps bringing in even more formidable
game animals from other parts of the galaxy.
Thelon began to notice individual differences
among them. But seldom did a week go by without
a hunt. Death was only a matter of time against
such monstrous quarry, but there could be no

hanging back. Two hunts were especially challenging, in different ways.

In a plateau region somewhere in the west, Thelon found himself sent with the hunting pack after a gigantic flightless bird. The creature stood over eleven feet high with a monstrous beak nearly a third as long. But unlike any of the other animals they had hunted, this one was hard to distract. No matter what tactics were used, the gigantic bird would single out one member of the pack and run him down. A girl who had been right next to him was caught from behind and literally bitten in half.

But the thing that most disturbed Thelon was the delay of the Hunters in trying to net the creature. It was as if they enjoyed the sport of seeing one of the pack trying to outrace the flightless monster. Not even against the giant reptiles of the swampland were so many brought down.

The other challenge was more to his will than his hunting prowess. When the portal of the skycraft cone slid open he found himself racing across the Barren Lands. The temptation to tear off his collar and just keep running almost overcame him. The Anomaly was not many miles away; he could see the protecting forest stretching across the horizon. But there was no chance of taking Brenda with him, and his escape might even have endangered the Anomaly itself. When the wailing alarm sounded, he loped back to his stall with the rest of the hunting pack.

It was this experience that steeled his will to go on. His quest was still unfulfilled, and there was much about the Hunters that he did not know. The double ordeal of removing his collar and then easing through the sting-fence sealing the kennel was a severe test. So severe that it would be many days before he could again bring himself to face it. But tonight he was free.

He crept past the opening of the females' kennel. Over thirty of the swift, long-legged girls lay sleeping in hammocks hung from the metal walls; but he could not distinguish Brenda in the dim light. There was no alarm. The Hunters were so confident of their security system that no drover machines appeared. Thelon moved freely through the immense structure.

The Hunters never sat or lay down; inside the shielding metal walls of a skycraft or here inside their main base they moved with a strange flowing motion. As far as he knew they never slept. He came upon two of them facing each other across some kind of elaborate game stage. They wore light shimmering garments, unlike the protective clothing they wore outside. They were both silent and absolutely motionless, so entranced by their mental contest that they were oblivious of the human being nearby who was no less entranced with them. At first glance Thelon had taken them for statues.

They were leprous white, much larger than a human being; but they did not seem to have any definite skeletal structure, as if they could assume almost any shape they chose. This was the first time he had ever seen them without their protective clothing. They had eyes, or visual receptors of some kind, in the fleshy protuberances at the top of their main bulk; there was also a kind of lipless maw, but no sign of ears, nose, or hair. They reminded Thelon vaguely of some kind of giant mollusk. The game stage rose nearly as high as themselves, nearly filling the alcove where they stood.

At first he had assumed that it was merely a three-dimensional variant of chess. Only slowly did its inhuman complexity dawn on him. There were three levels through which the pieces could move, with five times as many pieces and at least twice the number of positions on each level as in chess. The Hunters somehow controlled the movement of the pieces; although they themselves remained absolutely silent and motionless.

Then he realized that the pieces were all continually evolving in color, and hence probably in value and capability as well. Thus the game was being played in four dimensions, not just three. All Thelon understood about it was that it was clearly beyond human understanding.

He was just about to slip away when the positions and colors of the pieces suddenly froze. The two Hunters turned and glided across the alcove, and a kind of sideboard emerged from the metal wall. It was covered with exquisite little bowls filled with liquids of various colors and consistencies.

Their "hands" were amazingly dextrous appendages, seemingly able to assume any desired shape. It was like watching a mitten turn into a glove and then back again each time they picked up one of the delicate little bowls and slowly ingested its contents. Thelon was certain that they were somehow conversing, although neither made the faintest sound.

Then the contest was resumed. For hours? Days? Weeks? Thelon slipped silently away, leaving the two aliens to their inhumanly complex game. He still had no real idea of the size or location of the vast structure, or how many Hunters and skycraft were based here. Nor could he even guess at the number of human beings he might find. But if those killed were continually being replaced with specially bred and trained adults, then there must be nurseries somewhere. He wondered if there were other special breeds of human beings.

The lights of the kennel were already beginning to brighten with artificial dawn as he hurried back. The ordeal of passing once more through the sting-fence brought him to the limit of his psychological resources. He badly needed sleep.

But hardly had he climbed into his hammock and replaced his collar than the wailing alarm sounded the hunt. His eyes smarting from lack of sleep, he could only rise and trot obediently along with the rest of the pack into the yawning portal of the skycraft cone.

It was a day of horror. Never before had so many splendid young men and women been so wantonly sacrificed to the inhuman sport of the Hunters. But for once he had an advantage over the rest of the hunting pack.

There was a bluish fringe along the horizon that may have been mountains, but as far as the eye could see there stretched only a vast burning ocean of sand. His greater strength carried him more easily over the rolling dunes than his swifter but weaker companions. In fact, he had never seen the hunting pack move so slowly, so reluctantly.

He had no idea what kind of creature they were hunting. His eyes swept the desert sands for any sign of life; but there was none. That was when he noticed that the others kept looking down at the sand itself. Brenda made a sign with her hand like a snake or centipede crawling, then pointed down. Thelon drew a deep breath. Whatever they were after lived in the sand, and he knew it would be huge and deadly.

Their very step was undermined by the dry, shifting sands. The three Hunters standing in a line beside their netting machines were swathed in extra-heavy garments, thick and rubbery. All at once there was a cry to his right, and the pack scattered. All but two girls, who struggled frantically as the dry sand fell away beneath them in an ever widening funnel.

He ran to the brink of the funnel. Despite their cries and struggles, the girls were slipping slowly downwards. He dived onto his stomach and just managed to grab the closest girl by the wrist and pull her to safety. The other girl had slid nearly to the bottom of the funnel, and he started to climb over the side after her.

"Tullen! No!" cried Brenda, darting forward and grabbing his arm.

There was a scream of terror from below. The bottom of the funnel opened and a hideous yellow head, like that of some enormous maggot, pushed itself into the air. It seized the screaming, struggling girl and began devouring her as leisurely as a caterpillar devouring a leaf.

Thelon stared in horror. He hardly noticed the
throbbing wail from the skycraft cone. Only
Brenda's frantic tugging at his arm saved him
from the rain of filaments that dropped into the
funnel.

Either the aim was off or the huge head had
withdrawn from the bottom before the mass of
stinging filaments hit, but the funnel was empty
when he again looked over the brink. The writhing
tangle of filaments suddenly went dead. Once
more there arose a throbbing wail from the
skycraft cone. Once more the hunting pack
plodded reluctantly across the burning sands.

Thelon looked back with a hatred such as he had
never known. The Hunters were not so much
trying to position this monster as using the
hunting pack as bait. They were fishing in a sea of
sand, and the nets could only be cast while the bait
was being devoured.

Four times the net was cast; four times the
monster escaped — if indeed it was the same
creature each time. Eleven young men and women
had already died hideously, and still the throbbing
wail urged them onwards. Then Thelon himself
felt the earth suddenly give way beneath him; but
his powerful legs, driving like pistons into loose
sand, carried him to safety. A young man nearby
was not so lucky. But again the net failed.

The sand, the sun, and the constant fear were
also taking their toll. On and on the hunting pack
plodded without rest, zigzagging up and back
across the dunes. Was there only one monster, or
many? Three more died hideously, and still the
nets failed.

While trying unsuccessfully to rescue a girl who had been trapped in a funnel, he got a closer look at the monster. The maggot-like head was over six feet across; around it writhed a horrid mane of tentacles, which it used for both digging and clutching its prey. Then the throbbing wail warned him to scatter with the rest of the pack.

He kept telling himself that it could not go on much longer. But still the Hunters stood outside the portal of the skycraft cone; still the great mother ship hovered in the cloudless sky above. It seemed that the hunt would continue until either the quarry had been netted or the entire hunting pack devoured. Then once again he was scrambling for his life as the sand started to fall away beneath his feet.

He did not see who was caught this time, but the instant his feet touched solid ground he whirled and dived back toward the brink in hopes of grabbing the victim's hand or wrist. But he was too late; the girl had already slipped out of reach, doomed to a hideous death. She looked helplessly up at him. It was Brenda!

He leaped over the brink; sliding and skidding down the collapsing wall of the funnel, he reached her side. He grabbed her around the waist, and together they clawed and churned their way upward through the avalanche of burning sand. His thighs screamed in agony, his ankles felt like they would snap from the strain, but still the funnel continued to widen. Then one side of it hit the base of a dune, and for a moment the sand did not fall so fast. With a last effort they dragged themselves over the brink.

Then they were on their feet and running for their lives. Frustrated by its prey, the monster had at last been lured into the open. It moved swiftly, but not swiftly enough. The remainder of the hunting pack surrounded it, dodging, leaping, and jabbing at it with their daggers.

Rising twenty feet above them like some colossal sea anemone, the nightmare creature crashed down onto the sand, trying to crush its tormentors beneath its tremendous bulk. Then the throbbing wail echoed across the burning sands and the hunting pack scattered, many actually staggering from exhaustion. A deadly rain of filaments fell all about the monster.

Never had the sound of recall been so welcome. The hunting pack, now cruelly depleted, turned their backs on the obscene carcass and trotted obediently back toward their stalls in the skycraft cone. Gangs of gorilla-men were already carrying their usual assemblage of spools, metal beams, and rollers that they used for recovering the quarry. But the look of hatred on Brenda's face was something new. She had at last realized that she was a human being.

That night Thelon slept as soundly as the rest of the hunting pack, and napped a good part of the following day. Replacements had brought them up to full strength again. The hunt had been successful — no matter what it had cost in human life and suffering. To the Hunters, that was all that mattered.

But he did not know even where to begin fighting back. Fire? Explosives? He had no idea. But something, anything; even if it was only a feeble gesture of defiance. The following night he again left his kennel.

But as he crept past the females' kennel, Brenda darted out of the corner. She stared at him expressionlessly for a moment; then tried to open her collar. The shock sent her reeling. Thelon shook his head, beckoning her to remain. He might bring himself to face the ordeal of opening her collar; but there was no way he could get her through the sting-fence. There was a hurt look in her jade-green eyes as he disappeared up a ramp.

All that night he roamed at will through the vast structure without reaching its outer walls; it was possibly several miles square. A reasonable caution protected him from the dull senses of the Hunters. But though he looked everywhere he could find no means of destruction.

He came upon a row of kennels filled with human children, separated according to age and sex. A complex of machines serviced them; but there were also several gorilla-men nearby, and he dared not come any closer. He spent the rest of the night exploring in another direction.

From a ramp leading back to his kennel he looked down into a room drenched with violet light. Below him a battery of machines were stuffing the desert monster. In one corner stood a giant reptile; nearby stood the gigantic flightless bird netted at the cost of so many lives. Both were already stuffed and held in stout metal frames by networks of filaments, ready for shipment into space. Trophies of the planet earth.

Thelon was slowly becoming inured to the ordeal of leaving his kennel. The next time he left it he found Brenda standing just on the other side of the invisible sting-fence. He never knew the hours of pain and despair she had endured trying to remove her collar. But still she could only watch him with hurt eyes as he disappeared from sight.

In a burst of passion she finally wrenched the collar from her neck. But the sting-fence almost knocked her unconscious when she tried to plunge through it. One of the hunting pack awoke and watched her drowsily for a moment or two; then went back to sleep. But Brenda did not sleep. She paced restlessly back and forth inside the invisible barrier like a jungle cat. She did not like to fail.

Meanwhile Thelon moved continually upward. If he could not discover the outer dimensions of the structure, he could at least find out how high it stood. Ramp followed ramp for several hundred feet, until at last he came to a heavy metal door. It opened at a touch, and for a moment he thought he was beneath the open sky. There were no walls as far as he could see in the dim light. But then he became aware of a faint luminescence far overhead. It was a hangar.

The hangar deck must have covered at least two or three square miles; although it was hard to judge in the dim light. Then he began to discern vast shapes hanging motionless in the air; row upon row of skycraft, each being serviced by a swarm of machines like worker bees about their queen. But all the skycraft were truncated at one end, the cones evidently somewhere lower down in the structure.

His collar was being monitored back in the

kennel, and if there were any drover machines in the vast structure they were apparently not activated by only one or two humans on the loose. But he did not know what other defenses might be lurking here. He had not forgotten the room with the violet light. He hugged the side wall, where huge grounding cables curved into the deck plates like buttresses. There were doors here.

He had covered perhaps a third of the distance across the hangar when he heard a faint humming sound. Crouching behind a grounding cable he looked upward. And there were the stars! The gap in the roof was rapidly widening. Then an enormous shape glided silently down out of the night sky. The skycraft settled into line with the others, and a cone section broke away and dropped through an opening in the hangar deck that had not been there a moment ago. When he looked up again the stars were gone.

It was time for him to be gone as well. Dawn was not many hours away; and though it would probably be several days yet before the pack hunted again, he decided to return to the kennel. He had seen enough for one night; perhaps too much. The power of the Hunters was overwhelming. For all he knew they were the greatest force in the galaxy. How could he even hope to be more than a moment's nuisance to them? Perhaps he should have escaped when he had the chance.

He had marked his route, and had no trouble finding his way back. It was still well before dawn, but Brenda was up and waiting for him. They stood face to face, separated by the invisible wall of pain; her jade-green eyes held some mysterious triumph. Then he noticed that her collar was gone. Proudly, she held it up for him. He knew all too well the agony she must have endured, and he smiled encouragingly at her.

Then the wailing alarm startled them. A hunt? At this hour? They never hunted at night, and had always been given at least a few days to recuperate. Brenda gestured frantically toward the skycraft cone looming in the darkness above them; her voice sounded strange and distant, muffled by the sting-fence. He raced back to his kennel.

A jolt of pain hit him as he started to ease into the sting-fence; but then it ceased. The fence was down. He rushed to his hammock through the welter of young men moving obediently toward their stalls in the skycraft cone. Snatching up his collar, he rushed after them.

CHAPTER XIV: TIMOTHY

The hunting pack had been trained since infancy to respond to each pitch of the throbbing siren, just as human beings had once trained dogs. The Hunters themselves evidently could not hear the sound. Thelon could hear it; although he still did not understand the meaning of the signals. But he was certain that he had never heard this particular pitch before.

Deceleration had been so fast that the network of filaments holding him in his stall had been stretched several feet. Now he found himself fanning out in a wide circle with the rest of the hunting pack. It was still night; although the eastern horizon looked somewhat less black than the rest of the sky. What kind of monster could they hunt in the dark?

The hunting pack dashed back and forth, yelping and crying like hounds on the scent.

Thelon followed Brenda, shouting and dashing back and forth with the rest. Once he ran smack into the giant face of a drover machine, standing like some hideous idol in the slowly graying light. Then something whizzed past his ear. An arrow? A bullet? He kept running.

In the first light of dawn he became aware of precise, machine-tended fields of grain and vegetables stretching into the distance all around him. This was evidently where their food was grown. Hundreds of men, women and children were being driven together in the center of the field by a ring of gorilla-men armed with long electric prods. Somehow these people had deactivated the drover machines and raided the fields of the Hunters, and probably not for the first time.

They were not wildmen; one glance told Thelon that. But recall sounded before he could get a closer look, and he had to hurry back to his stall. He never saw when the net landed.

Despite his weariness and the will-sapping shocks of the previous night, he was determined to find out who these people were and what had become of them. If one kind of machine could be deactivated, why not another? He slipped out of his kennel the moment the lights dimmed.

Brenda was waiting for him. She had already succeeded in removing her collar; but the sting-fence still defeated her. He tried to show her how to ease her way through the invisible barrier, rather than throwing herself against it. But she still could not endure the pain. He had to leave her behind.

The kennels where the replacements for the

hunting pack were raised seemed the logical place
to begin his search; nearly all the human beings he
had seen thus far had been housed in that vicinity.
Hundreds of replacements lay asleep in their
hammocks, from toddlers up to fully-trained
adults. All wore the same gray-green leather
tunics; all had unusually lithe bodies and long
legs. The machines servicing their kennels ignored
him. Without his collar, they did not know of his
existence.

There were no gorilla-men present tonight; evidently they had other work to do. Further on he
came to their kennels. There must have been fully
a thousand of them curled uncouthly in their stout
hammocks. Not one of them weighed less than
three hundred pounds. A few watched him as he
passed, but their eyes were dull and incurious.

He came upon two Hunters in an alcove playing
their four-dimensional game. In a larger alcove he
saw no less than seventeen of them standing in a
silent ring like the monoliths of Stonehenge. It
was probably a conference of some kind, although
not the least twitch or whisper escaped from
them. Nor did their dull senses detect him as he
crept past on an overhead ramp. He had already
searched a half mile of ramps, halls, kennels, and
alcoves; but there was still no sign of the captives.

He started down a broad ramp, but was checked
by the sight of a group of Hunters. They were
gliding leisurely about a large circular hall,
critically examining the contents of a ring of open
cages. He crept to a position where he could see
what they were looking at. The sight came as a
revelation.

Despite their incredible technology, the Hunters had evidently not overcome the primitive instincts of their race. Perhaps netting monstrous creatures simulated the challenges overcome by their distant ancestors on their home planet. Nor had they lost their primitive love of the grotesque.

He had read of human freaks and monstrosities being born from time to time. He had also read how people had once bred bizarre goldfish; how charlatans had manufactured human freaks for exhibition at fairs by keeping children locked in devices that distorted their natural growth. But the human grotesqueries below could not have been produced in any such manner. Somehow their genetic structure had been tampered with. The Hunters moved from cage to cage like connoisseurs at an art exhibition.

He turned away in disgust, moving up the ramp to a higher level. The Hunters seemed more numerous here; the number and complexity of their machines also seemed to increase. But there was still no sign of the captives.

He had grown confident of his ability to escape detection, moving through the defenses of the enemy like a shadow. But just before ascending a long ramp he happened to glance behind him. Brenda was standing not ten feet away. He had neither seen nor heard her cat-like approach. She had at last overcome the ordeal of the sting-fence. But how had she found him?

The question must have been written on his face, for she pointed at him and whispered, "Clomp, clomp, clomp!"

Apparently his movements had not been quite so

shadow-like as he believed. But even her keen ears
could not have heard him at any great distance.
She must have done some searching before getting
close enough to hear him.

He started to pantomime the netting that
morning in the cornfields, but she caught on
before he had even finished. Beckoning him to
follow, she turned and led him back the way he
had come. Her route was less direct, but she
moved much more swiftly than he had. Twice she
warned him about "clomping."

When they reached the last ramp leading to the
kennels, Brenda went up instead of down. The
long ramp spiraled round and round the tapering
hull of the skycraft cone.

Each level held a kind of dock, which could be
extended outwards from the ramp for loading and
unloading that section. Brenda had seen him
disappear up this very ramp. When she had come
searching for him she had apparently followed it
to the top, beyond where he himself had left it.
They halted on the fourth level above the kennels.

There were over three hundred captives; men,
women, and children. They were dressed in simple
garments of homespun cloth. Most of them were
sleeping, huddled together in the center of a large
hall. Around them stood a ring of gorilla-men
armed with long electric prods. Something was
wrong here.

Spacious kennels lined one whole side of the
hall; but they were all empty. Machines worked
busily at the places from which the sting-fences
were projected. The drover machines in the hall
were as dead as the ones he had seen that morning

in the cornfield.

Then he noticed a solitary figure sitting Indian-fashion near the center of the huddle. The pale young man squinted through myopic eyes, searching for some means of escape. Thelon could see at a glance that there was no chance of that. But why weren't these people in the kennels? And what had happened to the drover machines?

Brenda touched his arm, and led the way back down to the nearest dock. It had been extended outwards, and a portal stood open in the hull of the skycraft cone. Thelon peered warily inside. There were several gorilla-men lugging one of the huge netting machines toward the dock. Then one of them turned and saw him.

There would be no problem eluding these clumsy brutes. But what if they sounded the alarm? For several moments the gorilla-man stared dully at him; then he slowly raised his paw to his throat. The collars worn by the gorilla-men were heavier than those worn by the hunting pack. Thelon wondered if they also gave a heavier jolt.

In past days he had also wondered if the gorilla-men might somehow be organized in resistance against the Hunters. Their physical strength was prodigious; but they seemed so mindless and docile — mere beasts of burden — that he had quickly abandoned this idea.

The gorilla-man turned and grunted, and six others shambled after him out onto the dock. Thelon poised himself to dodge in any direction should they try to capture him.

Then he realized that it was not him they were staring at. Brenda was perched insolently on the

railing of the ramp just above them. She had never
learned how to smile or laugh; but there was no
mistaking the mockery in her jade-green eyes. She
pointed tauntingly to her own naked throat.

There were two transformations within as many
seconds. The gorilla-men suddenly exploded with
anger; then just as suddenly were docile again, as
if they had all been knocked nearly senseless by
some invisible blow. Thelon now understood the
purpose of the heavier collars. Perhaps they were
not so docile as he had thought; but only kept that
way through constant monitoring.

Dawn was approaching, and soon both he and
Brenda would have to return to their respective
kennels. More important, autumn was approaching; the Hunters would soon be moving to their
African station, leaving only their machines
behind them. He had no idea what kind of
creatures he would have to face in Africa; but he
knew that he was the slowest of the hunting pack,
the oldest and least agile. Could he really hope to
survive the entire hunting season?

Escape and try to find the people who sent radio
messages to the Cave Cities? Perhaps he could
work out some plan with Brenda, now that she
was able to leave her kennel at night. Ideas raced
through his mind. But he could think of no
rational solution; nothing better than some kind of
suicidal gesture, and his reason told him that any
damage he might do would be repaired by the
machines of the Hunters within hours, perhaps
minutes. All resistance seemed futile, irrational.
Then the impulse of a young girl answered all his
questions, committing him irrevocably.

Brenda suddenly jumped down from the railing and strode fearlessly right into the midst of the gorilla-men, an insulting mockery in her jade-green eyes. Before Thelon could stop her, she stepped right up to a great shambling brute weighing a good four hundred pounds and removed his collar. The other gorilla-men began jabbering excitedly.

She turned her back on them and returned slowly to the railing. Thelon alone noticed that she staggered slightly, that there was a glassiness about her eyes. The stunning, mind-boggling jolt of pain she had endured without flinching was the greatest effort of will power he had ever witnessed. It was several minutes before she could turn around again; but when she did the mockery was back in her eyes. She twirled the gorilla-men's collar around her finger, taunting the others.

The scene that followed might have been comical, had not the issue been so vital to the planet earth. The gorilla-men tugged at their collars, and were sent reeling; then they started to get angry, and were instantly jolted back into docility again. Brenda mocked at their every failure, goading them on.

At last, trembling with anger, the brute whose collar she had removed grabbed one of the others and tore away his collar (and almost his head as well). Two were now free, and moments later all seven. Staggering from shock, they were in imminent danger of plunging to their deaths over the sides of the railless dock.

Thelon realized that he was now committed to action. Through some strenuous pulling and pushing he got the gorilla-men safely onto the ramp. Then he got them moving toward the hall where the captives were being held. Brenda had opened the floodgates. There was no turning back.

The machines repairing the sting-fences ignored them; the giant faces of the drover machines glared at them, but they had been deactivated. The gorilla-men with the electric prods began to shamble ominously toward them. When they realized that they were not wearing collars, an excited jabbering arose all about the hall.

Brenda continued to goad the freed gorilla-men, leading them about to remove the collars of the others. Soon she had a whole troop of the great brutes shambling after her. Some were so stunned by repeated shocks that they walked into walls and fell headlong over the railings; but she kept them moving. Their dull minds were inured to obedience. But how long would the mood last?

Thelon set them to work hauling the deactivated drover machines out of the hall and cleaning up the mess. Their natural emotions had been stunted since infancy, and he knew that it would not take much to ignite them into an explosion of rage.

"Why are you doing that?" asked a meek voice.

It was the pale young man who had been sitting Indian-fashion at the center of the huddle; he was standing now, and his puny frame was not much more robust than that of a boy. He squinted up at Thelon with myopic eyes.

"To keep them busy," he answered, increasingly concerned with the mood of the gorilla-men. The other captives still cringed from them.

"Ah, so you can talk," said the young man. "I rather suspected that you could. Yes, by all means keep them busy. That will keep them from thinking — though I doubt that they are capable of any real degree of cerebration — while we determine our next move." There was an almost simpleminded look on his homely face. "Now about their collars. We've often wondered, unfortunately without sufficient data, whether —"

"Did you lead the raid on the cornfields yesterday?" Thelon looked curiously at him. Whatever else this puny young man was, he was obviously intelligent. Somebody had deactivated the drover machines. And the sting-fences of the kennels?

"Lead? Me? Oh, no! No one ever follows me. I just neutralized the watchdogs. That is, the guard mechanisms set by the extraterrestrials to apprehend intruders. I wonder how they did detect us this time. But I suppose their devices really are quite sophisticated. Perhaps you know? Judging by your apparel, would I be correct in surmising that you're one of those who cut off our escape? Remarkably swift. Though not in a good cause, if you'll pardon my saying so. And you can talk, which our studies lead us to believe —"

"Did you also deactivate these machines?" Thelon pointed to the drover machines being hauled out by the gorilla-men.

"Yes, indeed. Quite simple, really. You see, their power supplies, while compact and remarkably sophisticated — "

"Did you also deactivate the sting-fences?"

"Sting-fences?" The young man looked puzzled. "What are . . . Ah, I have you! You mean the force fields?" He grinned. "Yes, I suppose they do sting, and they certainly are a kind of fence, albeit a sub-atomic one. Sting-fences, eh? That's really grand." He waggled his head in appreciation.

"But can you deactivate them?" Thelon insisted.

"Yes, indeed. In fact, they're even simpler . . . . By the way, what do you call yonder mechanisms, the ones with the large painted faces?"

"Drover machines." Thelon felt himself beginning to blush.

"Drover machines, eh? That's very, uh, descriptive. And sting-fences? You know, I've often pondered on the dissemination of language, how it arises when . . . ."

Thelon left him talking. "Brenda!" he cried, racing across the hall.

Her troop of gorilla-men had by now been shocked into stupor. But she kept them moving with slaps, kicks, punches, and even a nip or two with her dagger, removing the last of the collars. At a signal from Thelon she herded them toward the nearest ramp. Then he raced back and grabbed the young man by the arm, interrupting his soliloquy.

Most of the hunting pack were still asleep when they reached the kennels. Brenda had nearly a score of stupefied gorilla-men in her troop, and she had to circle them like a sheepdog to keep them from wandering off or walking into walls. Thelon set the young man to work on the sting-fences.

And it was as easy as he had said. He simply attached a small metal ring to one side of the opening; then made some adjustments inside a control panel in the opposite wall which Thelon had not known existed. It would probably set off some kind of alarm, but that could not be helped.

Getting the males uncollared and out of the kennel was no problem. The females were another matter. They were more numerous, and far less inclined to take orders from Brenda. She had learned much since Thelon had rescued her; but not tact. There were some daggers drawn before he was able to restore order. They had to be safely out of the area before the drover machines started arriving.

The myopic young man agreed. "The extraterrestrials are quite powerless without their machines. At least, I believe they are. All our reports say that they themselves, while of formidable stature, are quite slow and uncoordinated. Like a man under water, I suppose."

"They move fast enough in here," said Thelon hurriedly. "Perhaps too fast. We'll worry about what it all means later. Right now we have work to do."

Kennel after kennel was liberated, and Thelon grew increasingly anxious about how the Hunters would respond. The young man had deactivated every defense system so far, but how much longer could it last? And how much longer could they keep the liberated gorilla-men under control? The nervous systems of those in Brenda's troop were now probably frazzled beyond recovery, and they shambled dumbly after her from kennel to kennel. But the hundreds of others no longer had collars to keep them docile.

There were nearly a thousand human beings now concentrated in the great hall. Thelon felt increasingly like his ancestor, Walter Carswell. He too struggled against overwhelming odds, against both the inhuman power of the Hunters and the savagery of his own kind. Walter Carswell had led his people to the safety of the darkness. He himself wanted desperately to regain the light. But he too had little choice but just to keep moving, without any set purpose or direction. To stand was to die, in one hideous way or another. There were probably rooms with violet lights all over the hemisphere.

He had posted scouts, seen to it that the liberated did not leave their kennels until their collars had been removed, and kept the noise and confusion to a minimum. Only a few drover machines had appeared, and the myopic young man had deactivated these. But he was fast losing control of the gorilla-men, and there was no way of reducing their numbers. The best thing he could do now was to increase their numbers, enormously.

At the first sign of artificial dawn he set the people to barricading the ramps and portals leading into the hall. Barricades would not stop the Hunters or their machines, but they might impede the gorilla-men, for a while. The gorilla-men themselves he led away from the hall in a screaming, rampaging horde, including Brenda's stupified collar-openers. Brenda herself hurried the myopic young man along in their wake.

"My dear young woman," he protested. "There's

no call for you to pull my hair. And you needn't pinch me like that, if you please. I'm not robust. And all this howling and grimacing is rather disconcerting. Why, these fellows act just like apes! They even look that way."

But the look in her jade-green eyes silenced him, and he trotted obediently along at her side, encouraged by an occasional cuff.

Thelon set him at once to opening the kennels. These were few in number; but there were hundreds of gorilla-men in each, all wide awake. By the time the young man had deactivated the last sting-fence he was so terrified by the noise and confusion that he almost looked like one of Brenda's collar-openers.

"Brenda!" Thelon beckoned to her through the savage din, as he grabbed the myopic young man by the arm. The three of them escaped up a ramp.

The hall behind them was already a pandemonium of crazed gorilla-men wildly snatching at collars, failing or succeeding in wrenching them off, trying again and again, howling like maddened demons as they worked themselves into a rage, were stunned back into docility (those that still wore collars), and then worked themselves into a rage again. They had raced out of their kennels the instant the sting-fence was down, and the drover machines were now gathering from all over the vast structure. The crazed gorilla-men attacked them with metal bars and beams, or just their own fists. So far the machines were losing.

"That was harrowing," sighed the myopic young man when they were safely inside the barricades again. "Rather uncomfortably dynamic," he added, as Brenda moved off through the crowd. "But you know of course that your gang of thugs, devastating as they may now seem, are no match for . . . . Oh, by the way," a new thought struck him. "It seems that none of these people can talk after all. I approached several of them, but it was like trying to converse with a stone. However did you yourself . . . ." Then another new thought struck him. "You know, I don't even know your name. Assuming, of course, that you have one. Which, by the bye, may be a gross assumption, considering that . . . . In any case, my name is Timothy Peebles VII. Glad to meet you, I'm sure."

"My name is Thelon, and I am certainly glad to have met you, Timothy. What else do you know about these machines? Could you, for instance, fly one of the skycraft?"

"Skycraft? I presume you mean . . . . That's not bad. Though not nearly so vivid as *sting-fence*, or even *drover* machine. But as to flying one, yes. Given time. In fact, I've always wondered how they worked. The *skycraft*, as you call them. Presumably by some occult energy form. Antimatter? Electomagnetism? I wonder. But then, that might account for all this shielding —"

"Wait here, Timothy!" Thelon dived into the midst of the crowd that now swarmed all about them.

By dint of some hard pushing and shoving, he at last worked his way across the hall to where Brenda stood, dagger drawn, glaring back at several females of the hunting pack who had gathered angrily around her.

"Brenda, no!" he said firmly, leading her back through the crowd. Surprisingly, she did not resist.

He had set her and several of the captives to try and bring some order to the huge throng. But the females of the hunting pack still did not like taking orders from her. Nor was she very tactful in giving them. She was safer by his side.

Thelon felt more strongly than ever that he had lost control of events. It was like a boulder tipped over the side of a hill, moving slowly at first but all the while gathering momentum until at last nothing can stop it — least of all the one who tipped the boulder in the first place. The whole vast structure seemed to resound with the cries and howls of the rampaging gorilla-men, the crash of battle as they attacked and were attacked by the machines of the Hunters. But where were the Hunters themselves?

Then he heard a new sound, softer and more ominous. Metal doors began to close all about them, seeming to emerge from the very walls. The ramps and portals leading into the hall were sealed off, and he could hear the same thing happening in every direction. The Hunters were evidently segregating the danger, as they might have with a fire or flood.

"Ah," said Timothy, grinning. "I see what they're up to. They're not fools, you know. But you needn't look so anxious about the doors, I'm sure I can open them again. The real problem is what do we do then. You wouldn't happen to know of an exit, would you, uh, Thelon? Oh, by the way," a new thought struck him. "I just remembered

something I wanted to ask you. Is your name —
which is a rather unusual one, though no offense
meant when I say that, I assure you — spelled T-H-
E-L-O-N? It is? Like the river that —"

"Yes, I'm from the region of the Thelon River.
My people have lived there for centuries in a
magnetic anomaly. But that's not important now.
How do we get out of here? That's the question."

But the young man only stared at him, his weak
eyes blinking rapidly, as if he had just met with
some startling revelation. "Why, of course!" he
cried. "A magnetic anomaly! And you told me that
they move about easily in here, while they are
morbidly slow and uncoordinated . . . Of course!
Why should non-humans, actually non-earthlings,
have a central nervous system like . . . Or commun-
icate in any way . . . . But that explains all this
heavy shielding!"

He then began rambling on and on about "psy-
fields," "telepathy," "synchronicity," "psycho-
kenesis," and strangely enough, something
about "slime molds." Thelon had heard of telepathy, but only as a form of communication
between individuals, not intercommunication between the various parts of the same individual.
But were the Hunters really individuals, and not,
say, conglomerate beings of some kind?

The important thing now was that they were beginning to respond. The raging gorilla-men would
soon be mopped up, and perhaps a few minor
adjustments made in the programming of the
machine complex. Then the Hunters would leave
for Africa on schedule. The only result of all this
would probably be that every room with violet

lights on the North American continent would be well stocked for winter. Their machines were just too powerful.

"Ah, but Thelon," said Timothy. "A human mind can always defeat mere machines. A machine can answer questions, but it can't ask them. Ergo, it is necessarily passive. You see, Thelon —"

"I see nothing right now but their strength. You haven't been around this place as I have, Timothy. I don't know if there exists in the entire galaxy a superior force. Certainly not here on earth."

Timothy said thoughtfully, "The guiding principle in such a situation is clear enough. Intelligence can always defeat mere strength by turning that very strength against itself." He shrugged. "The application of the principle, however, is not —"

"The hangar!" cried Thelon. "That's where their real force is concentrated. Brenda, this way!"

CHAPTER XV: THE OPEN SKY

"These extraterrestrials can't think much of human intelligence," said Timothy, opening the last of a series of doors. "The principles of physics are universal, and it's all elementary if you know what you're looking for. There, that should —"

"Watch out!" cried Thelon, as Timothy began to open the door onto the hangar deck. "There's a drover machine stationed just outside."

Timothy shrugged. "Well, that makes sense. At least, from their point of view. The monkeys are out of their cages, so to speak. No offense meant, of course," he added quickly. "Just a figure of speech." He began fumbling through the pockets of his homespun jacket. "Ah, here it is. Now one of you will have to volunteer." And he explained what had to be done.

The giant face shot toward Thelon the instant he

stepped onto the hangar deck. The four metal claws grasped him; but Timothy had warned him not to struggle. Less than a hundred feet away the machine stopped dead and the claws released him.

"Now what?" said Timothy, stepping out from behind the giant face. "You still haven't told me why we're here."

"To look at a machine," Thelon replied, his eyes peering into the distance.

The hangar deck was now brightly lighted. Row upon row of skycraft, still being serviced by swarms of machines, stretched for miles. But there were no open spaces now, as if every skycraft on the planet had returned in response to the revolt. Every entrance onto the hangar deck was guarded by a drover machine.

"Oh, don't worry about them," said Timothy. "They won't attack unless we stray from the vicinity of this machine. As far as they know, it's captured us." He glanced over his shoulder. "I suppose you'll want to go back for the girl now. Quite beautiful, but I'm afraid rather uncomfortably dynamic. I've never seen eyes that color of green. And incredibly swift." He made some adjustments at the back of the drover machine. "There, now I have control of it. Hop aboard!"

Brenda shrank back into the portal as the drover machine sped straight for her, despite the fact that Thelon was perched on its mechanical arms. Timothy was out of sight, working the controls manually from behind. She seemed relieved when Thelon jumped down unharmed; even touching him affectionately, a thing she had never done before.

He had noticed that two of the skycraft were larger than any of the others; each over a quarter mile long. Beside one of them stood the stuffed desert monster, supported in a colossal metal frame by a network of filaments. Nearby, a crane was just now hoisting a similar frame containing a giant reptile up into the belly of the ship. These were trophies destined for the home planet. All the weaponry of the Hunters would be concentrated in these two cargo ships.

"See that large skycraft?" Thelon pointed.

Timothy squinted. "I'm afraid not. You see, my spectacles were broken when —"

"Just steer then. I'll guide you."

He and Brenda climbed into the mechanical arms of the drover machine, while Timothy operated the controls from behind the giant face. They sped like the wind across the hangar deck. None of the other drover machines so much as budged.

"We're almost there," cried Thelon. "Stop!"

Timothy took the order too literally, and Brenda was almost thrown to the deck. He climbed out from behind the giant face, muttering and rubbing his elbow. The look Brenda gave him sent him scurrying behind Thelon for protection and apologizing. But there was no time to lose.

"Quick, into the filaments," cried Thelon. "This looks like the last to be loaded."

He helped Timothy climb up into the network supporting the desert monster; then he started back for Brenda. But she was right behind him. The filaments were thin but immensely strong; they were also slightly elastic, like those that had held him in his stall in the skycraft. No sooner had they settled themselves than the crane lifted the huge metal framework upwards like a toy.

Another crane, smaller but more mobile, then carried them half the length of the spaceship. The next thing they knew they had been deposited in a cavernous hold among row upon row of stuffed and crated monsters.

Timothy gasped. "These aren't from earth, are they? Surely they're not the native fauna . . . But that's obvious. And you mean you actually hunted them?" He glanced uncomfortably at Brenda. "On foot? But then, I've often pondered the means by which the extraterrestrials bred human beings . . . ."

Half dragging, half carrying, Thelon got him down out of the filaments and moving toward the front of the ship. The rear was truncated, like all the other skycraft hovering just above the hangar deck; the cone was presumably moored somewhere lower down in the structure. Brenda's jade-green eyes darted suspiciously back and forth as they advanced; her hand was never far from the hilt of her dagger.

Thelon had only a vague idea of what he was looking for; but it seemed probable that any kind of weaponry the spaceship might have would be concentrated toward the prow. It was like a small city inside, and he had to keep a firm grip on Timothy's arm to keep him from gawking at the wonders they passed. Brenda looked only for possible enemies. The corridor opened at last onto a vast control deck.

"If you want me to fly this thing," said Timothy,

"I'll first have to get it out . . . . I wonder how these controls . . . . Why, they're all operated manually! But, then, they'd have to be, wouldn't they? I really should have anticipated this. But the telepathically operated controls below—"

Thelon interrupted, "I don't want you to try and fly this thing, even if it could be done." His eyes roamed over the incredible array of control panels. "What I'm looking for is a weapon, something we could use to blast our way out of here." And he described the force beam that had nearly destroyed them at the river bank.

"Ah, very good," Timothy approved. "A practical application of the principle of turning the strength of the strong against themselves. I never expected you to catch on so . . . . Ahem! That is to say, it sounds like a very good idea, Thelon. But how far is this hangar deck above ground? We seem to have climbed a long way."

"I'm not sure it is above ground. All I know is that above the roof lies the open sky. I've seen the stars at night. But I've never been able to find the limits of this colossal structure in any other direction. Look for some kind of weapon, Timothy. And if you can operate it, we'll try to blast an opening in one of the outer walls, perhaps in the roof itself."

Timothy nodded. "That seems sensible. Ah, what have we here?" Then he shook his head. "That can't be it. Lighting or heating probably . . . . Ah? No, not that either . . . ."

For the next twenty minutes he prowled and poked and squinted into everything. The controls were high off the floor, built for tall operators that never sat down, and sometimes he had to stand on tiptoes. He tended to linger over any machine or panel whose use he did not understand, even if it clearly had nothing to do with weaponry. Thelon had to keep him moving.

"Ah, here we are!" Timothy cried at last. "This may be what we're looking for."

He began fiddling with the controls, until a three-dimensional picture so vivid that it hurt the eyes flashed onto a round screen. It displayed the far wall of the hangar, through an immense flotilla of skycraft; there was a cross-thread pattern superimposed on the bottom of the screen. Systematically he began eliminating one control after another, trying to master the whole panel. At last he moved the cross-thread pattern to the very center of the screen and focused the picture on a skycraft nearby. Then he blithely twisted a knob.

Thelon blinked and rubbed his eyes. For a moment he thought that something was wrong with the picture. The skycraft had a gaping hole in its side twenty yards across, and there had not been a sound. It just dissolved!

"Try the outer wall, Timothy!" he cried. "Near the hangar deck. We still don't know where we are in relation to ground level."

The tight ranks of skycraft all around them required some deft maneuvering to get a clear shot. Then all at once there was a gaping hole in the outer wall; part of the hangar deck had also dissolved. Bright sunlight streamed through the opening. At least they were not underground. But how far were they above ground? If they were as far above ground as they were above the base of

the structure, then this was not a possible escape
route. There was only one way to find out.

"Wait here!"

Thelon dashed from the control center and back
along the corridor to the loading bay. It was a
good two hundred yards to the outer wall; but he
had dodged drover machines before. It was a fifty-
foot drop to the hangar deck.

Equipment and supplies were still being loaded;
but the crane's mechanical arms and tentacles
whipped about too fast for him to find a hold.
After a few minutes searching, he discovered a
chain in a nearby storage bin. It reached to within
nine or ten feet of the hangar deck.

He had not run twenty yards before the drover
machines began converging on him. Fluffy white
clouds scudded across the hole in the outer wall;
in the distance he could see a grove of trees. There
were three machines after him, and he would only
have time for a quick glance. The machines were
moving to pen him in; they did not know that the
opening existed.

It was a good twenty yards across. If the drop
was not too great, perhaps Timothy could rig
something with the crane to lower people to the
ground. Grabbing the side of the hole and leaning
out, Thelon glanced down — all of two feet. The
structure was almost entirely underground!

Leaping back, he just avoided the grasping
metal claws of the first machine; he quickly
dodged past the other two. He had covered nearly
a third of the distance back to the cargo ship
before they could wheel about and overtake him.
From then on it was two steps forward and one

step back, running and dodging and leaping. His last leap was for the chain, and he just managed to pull his legs out of reach of the metal claws. The giant faces glared at each other; but this was one contingency for which they had not been programmed.

Brenda was waiting for him at the top of the chain. She looked at him expressionlessly for a moment; and again reached out and gently placed her hand on his shoulder. This time Thelon kissed her, and she did not pull away.

In the control center they found Timothy busily removing panels from various cabinets near the screen. He grinned absent-mindedly up at them, obviously enjoying the prospect of some leisurely hours of tinkering and experimenting. He whistled softly to himself.

"Leave that for now, Timothy," Thelon said. "The hangar deck is almost at ground level, at the top of a steep hill. But you'll have to deactivate the drover machines before we can bring the people up here. That will take time, and we haven't any to spare."

"Ah, but I have the answer right here, you see." He giggled happily. "Really ingenious! As far as I can determine, it's the outer shell of the, uh, sky-craft that does both the aiming, via this screen, whose intensity, by the bye, I haven't yet discovered how to diminish — these extraterrestrials must have eyes even weaker than mine — and the actual firing. And from any point, in any direction. Watch!" And he blithely began disintegrating drover machines all over the hangar.

Thelon patted him encouragingly on the back.

"Keep it up until we get back, Timothy. We're going to try and bring all the others up from below."
Then a thought struck him. "When you've finished with the drover machines, see what you can do about damaging the other skycraft. It won't do us any good to escape if we're netted before we can get away."

Thelon and Brenda left him perched in front of the screen. He hardly waited for them to clear the hangar deck before he began to twist knobs, turn switches, and push buttons with increasing frenzy. His eyes slowly glassed over; there was a silly grin on his face, and his mind whirled at the thought of possessing such power. He, Timothy Peebles VII, vastly more powerful than any Thor or Zeus, hurling his thunderbolts. His head wobbled drunkenly as he continued to destroy everything in sight . . . .

The metal doors sealing off the ramps and portals leading into the hall below had saved the people there from the rampaging gorilla-men. The one open route up to the hangar deck had not yet been discovered. Savage howling and the clash of combat echoed from all sides of the vast structure. The people were glad to follow Thelon anywhere.

The hunting pack were as usual more skittish and temperamental; but Brenda tore into them like a Fury, kicking and punching and threatening with her dagger. This time not even the females fought back. They were the first to reach the hangar deck.

But there they were stymied. It seemed as if the world had returned to primordial chaos. The air literally crackled with energy; crippled machines ran amok; the walls, the hangar deck, and even the roof itself were rent with scores of gaping holes; the entire flotilla of skycraft lay in ruins. But still the force beams swept madly back and forth. Had Timothy lost his mind?

Thelon got the throng back down to a safer level, and arranged signals with Brenda. Then he was racing like the wind across the hangar deck, half expecting at any instant to be dissolved by a random force beam. The craters in the deck forced him to dodge this way and that; but he reached the cargo ship in one piece. The crane was still loading equipment and supplies.

He found Timothy bouncing up and down in front of the screen, giggling like a happy child, turning knobs and dials with abandon as he destroyed everything in sight. Thelon snatched him from his seat and shook him.

"Stop! Stop!" cried Timothy. "That's enough! Please! I'm all right now."

Thelon put him down, but kept an eye on him. "You did a good job, Timothy. I'm proud of you. They won't be following us with anything in this junkheap. Now take it easy for a minute. Breathe deeply. That's right."

The young man had started to cry, and his hands trembled. He nodded his head rapidly up and down.

"Yes, I'm fine now. Yes, indeed. I'll be all right now, so you needn't shake me any more. I really don't know how it ever —"

"Timothy! Watch out!" cried Thelon.

On the screen before them the hangar deck suddenly burst open, and a skycraft cone shot upward

from below. Before they could even move, the
whole prow of the cargo ship vanished in a tremendous burst of matter. Apparently there was
more than one control center on this ship, and the
Hunters had guessed wrong. It was a fatal mistake. The skycraft cone fell back through the deck,
blasted to rubble by Timothy.

Thelon wasted no time rushing to the front of
the ship; from its shattered prow he signaled to
Brenda across the ruins of the hangar deck. A moment later he saw a stream of frightened people
debouch from the portal and turn toward the nearest opening in the outer wall. Brenda kept them
moving, in no uncertain terms. But he could not
wait until they were gone. He was still worried
about Timothy going berserk again.

But he was only squinting myopically into a
mass of cables at the back of one of the control
panels. He seemed to be in full possession of his
faculties once more, and was never far from the
lighted screen. There were as many cone sections
moored somewhere below as there were ruined
skycraft up here on the hangar deck. Somehow
they had to be held off until Brenda had led the
others to the safety of the trees.

"Bring 'em on!" Timothy grinned, still
thoroughly enjoying the power he had learned to
wield. "Oh, don't worry, Thelon," he added quickly, afraid that he would be shaken again. "I'm
myself. But this spaceship is really a marvel. I
could hold off half a galaxy by merely pushing a
few buttons. And . . . . Oh, oh!" He jumped for the
controls.

The blast left a smoldering crater in the hangar

deck; the skycraft cone, which had barely emerged above the surface, collapsed ruins back into the structure. On one corner of the screen appeared scores of gorilla-men, still screaming and raging. In their blind fury they began attacking the machines that were still blindly servicing the rows of ruined skycraft. Timothy tinkered busily with the control panel.

"There!" He sat back, more like a happy child than ever. "That should do it! We just have to be out of here in, say, ten minutes after I turn this knob. Two hundred yards to the loading bay of the ship, the same distance to the outer wall — we shouldn't have any trouble. It's automatic, you see. The force beam will just sweep round and round. I've set it to start at the outer walls, then cycle inwards. Compute the area of the deck by the sweep speed of the force beam —"

"Tell me on the way. Just turn the knob and let's get out of here."

The crane continued to load the ship; swarms of machines continued to feed it from below and unload it from above. These latter, shuttling up and back inside the vast cargo ship, were easy to dodge. But Timothy balked at the chain and the sight of the fifty-foot drop to the hanger deck below.

"I'm afraid I forgot about how we were —"

"Just hold on!" Thelon cried. He descended the chain hand over hand with Timothy clinging to his back.

"Now what are you . . . you're not going to shake me again, are you? Remember, I'm not robust."

Thelon swung him bodily onto the back of the

drover machine they had used to get here. The three that had pursued him had evidently gone off to attack the gorilla-men, or been blasted out of existence by Timothy. The battle between the machines and the gorilla-men had grown furious, and the howls and crashing were getting closer.

"Get going!" Thelon cried, leaping onto the mechanical arms at the front of the giant face.

They reached the opening within seconds. But to Thelon's surprise the machine just kept going, sailing right through the gap and crashing down hard on the steep slope of the hillside. It stopped not fifty feet outside the wall. Jumping down from the metal arms, he found Timothy sprawled on his back. There was a silly look on his face.

"Yes," he mumbled, shaking his head dizzily, "you did say it was a hillside, didn't you. I'm afraid I forgot about that. There are no springs or shock-absorbers on these things. But it's almost impossible to overturn them. Probably some kind of gyro-system, or perhaps . . . ."

But the ten minutes were nearly up, and Thelon had seen enough of the power of the force beams to know that he wanted to be as far away as possible when they began to cycle. He set Timothy bodily on the back of the machine and once more climbed into its mechanical arms. He could see the refugees, a thousand men, women and children, straggling toward the trees in the distance. There was a river there, he could see it now.

Timothy's driving was not very good, and the giant face wove dizzily back and forth across the rolling plains. Then the earth beneath them began to tremble, and the drover machine came to a halt.

Thelon started to protest, but he too was curious about what was happening. He joined Timothy.

The roof of the shimmering gray-green structure covered several square miles at the summit of a small plateau; but it was nowhere more than the height of the hangar. Now it seemed to melt before their eyes; the roof and walls collapsed like heated wax, but at first there was no sound. Then the ground beneath them began to heave and sway as in an earthquake, and a dull grinding noise filled the air. The strength of the Hunters had been turned against them, and the whole vast structure began to collapse inwardly like the caldera of a volcano.

"You know," Timothy said thoughtfully. "It's really a pity in a way. There won't be much left here even to examine. And Africa is too far away ... For now, at least. But I wonder .... Oh, by the way, we're not far from home. Did I ever .... No, I don't think I ever did. Did I? In any case, it was a bomb shelter, long ago. Of Eddington Institute, which was once one of the most famous .... Did you know that when the extraterrestrials first came they had a lethal gas? You did? Well, Eddington Institute developed an antidote. Scientists had gathered from all over, you see, and they discovered that the combination .... But it was too late."

"Not if they return," said Thelon.

Timothy said doubtfully, "You know, after this, I don't think the planet earth will be very attractive for them. And you don't take revenge on animals, which, humiliating as it seems .... No, no, they won't be back. At least, I don't think so.

On the other hand, if they should return . . . . "

But Thelon was no longer listening. At the summit of a hill, silhouetted against the sky, he had spotted a slender, long-legged figure. The refugees had nearly reached the trees; but Brenda had stayed behind to wait for him.

"Why don't you catch up with the others, Timothy," he said. "But I think you'd better leave that drover machine behind. The sight of it coming toward them might frighten them."

"Oh, I'll warn them, turn it around and wave. Something like that. They'll know it's only . . . Besides, I've never had a chance to really dig into the power supply of these things. And don't they ever turn over? That's another fascinating question. You see, the weight distribution is all wrong, and yet they move with great speed over any kind of terrain . . . ." It was several minutes before he realized that he was talking to himself.

Thelon joined Brenda at the top of the hill, and there was a softness in her jade-green eyes that he had never seen before. They embraced as lovers. The sun poured down out of a sky free from terror for the first time in many generations of men. The trees were brilliant with autumn colors, and the small river ran like a ribbon of silver out onto the rolling plains.

The tasks before them seemed overwhelming; neither their children nor their children's children would see them completed. But with freedom all things are possible, and at least they had made a beginning. Then side by side they ran with long, loping strides beneath the open sky.